Kanishka

By

Devaguptapu Babu

 FriesenPress

Suite 300 - 990 Fort St
Victoria, BC, V8V 3K2
Canada

www.friesenpress.com

Copyright © 2021 by Devaguptapu Babu
First Edition — 2021

All rights reserved.

No part of this publication may be reproduced in any form, or by any means, electronic or mechanical, including photocopying, recording, or any information browsing, storage, or retrieval system, without permission in writing from FriesenPress.

ISBN
978-1-03-910598-0 (Hardcover)
978-1-03-910597-3 (Paperback)
978-1-03-910599-7 (eBook)

1. FICTION, ASIAN AMERICAN

Distributed to the trade by The Ingram Book Company

Table of Contents

Chapter One 1
Chapter Two 3
Chapter Three 12
Chapter Four 19
Chapter Five 23
Chapter Six 29
Chapter Seven 37
Chapter Eight 44
Chapter Nine 48
Chapter Ten 57
Chapter Eleven 69
Chapter Twelve 89
Chapter Thirteen 98
Chapter Fourteen 105
Chapter Fifteen 112
Chapter Sixteen 126
Chapter Seventeen 134
Chapter Eighteen 141
Chapter Nineteen 156
Chapter Twenty 170
Chapter Twenty-One 176

Dedicated to

My dear wife Padma who is my 'muse'
My Family
Raghu, Reema, Saamya, Keya
Priya, Greg, Naija and Nishta

About the Author

Devaguptapu Babu has been a professional engineer, a senior executive heading European operations for a major corporation, and a writer, director, and actor.

His North American theatrical journey started in 1968 at Cranbrook,BC. with "Finian's Rainbow".

In 1988 press in Manesha, WI. acclaimed, "He has succeeded in a monumental undertaking " Ramayana " which was a feather in his cap". In 2012 directed a play "EK" as well acted in the lead role in Austin, TX.

His first book, *Mystic* was published in 2016.

He has written many plays and *Kanishka* was developed from a one-man show he wrote, directed, and starred in to critical acclaim.

He and his wife live in Helotes, Texas.

Chapter One

First week in November 1988

It was evening. The sun was hovering on the western horizon with a kind of reddish hue. The sun was very tentative. He was unable to decide. On the one hand, he wondered if he should set himself down into the fast approaching night and let this very traveler trek all alone in the flaming heat of the hot sand dunes. On the other hand, not realizing that he was the reason for the boiling hot sand, he considered whether to keep the traveler company.

The dunes had been chiseled and carved by the mighty gusts of the wind. It is said that this sand storm is referred to as "aan-dhi" in some ancient, God-forsaken language, which we in the new world do not want to accept, lest our own grand 400-year-old classic heritage bite the dust. Hubble, the humble, keeps reminding us that the so-called black hole is in a topsy-turvy mode, expanding after an explosion 1200 billion light-years away in the non-comprehensible continuum of space. Since it happened 1200 billion years ago, the news is so old and dusty, the media ignore it. What a fall indeed for the major networks.

The sand dunes were lit up like burning flames. On one side, the setting sun was blasting his orange glow. The other side was like smoldering black coal with a kind of smoke emitting from it. The only disaccord in the setting was those footprints that were zig-zagging in the sands. The whole thing was like an impressionist painting with some unique elements like beat-up old clock-works, nitrate, and a yellow-tinted powder like sulfur in the man's transparent bag, which was from one of those high-end boutiques in London. Who in the hell would have a lunch pail like this? Was he an alien?

He relentlessly continued his sojourn through the Sahara. In the distance there was what looked like a North African city with its lights just going on. Luckily for this traveler he had a beacon to follow as the night was setting in. From the top of a minaret, the prayer call for the evening Namaz was heard.

Time is the only entity in the whole universe that seems permanent. It keeps its seconds ticking despite anything that surrounds it, be it a supernova or a black hole. It never ceases to tick. By any chance, is this what we call God? It is omnipresent, omniscient, and omnipotent in all respects. Time is the only thing that is not time-bound. It's all-powerful since it binds everything to its own time line and when the time comes, nothing can stop it. We try to quantify time in many different ways, but all are relative. Time seems to race for some unknown reason.

Chapter Two

Third week in August 2001

Along with her two kids, the blonde passenger in the jet-way proceeded to board the plane. The jet-way was about to be retracted as the ground agent bid the passengers a bon voyage to London. As soon as the final count was tallied, the standby passengers were to be boarded. There were only couple of people left in the gate area and a six-foot-tall English-looking gentleman was one of them. He had long, drawn-out facial features, along with a sharp nose. A black pipe in his mouth was clenched between his straight teeth, in more of a North American mode, but the pipe was still in the English style. He was wearing a long, black coat somewhat similar to the old English style, with a three-button, tweed sports jacket. A gold pocket watch was in his front pocket, with the gold chain looping in plain view of anyone talking to him. He was leaning on a square, white, Canadian-built, mass-produced pillar in New York's JFK International Airport and his eyes were fixed on a female passenger seated in the second row from the pillar.

She was a very slim young lady of an origin from either the South American side of the world or from the Mid-to-Near-East Asian side. Her features were sharp, with high cheekbones, and a very well-shaped nose complemented her round, dark eyes. Her well-groomed eyebrows were as jet-black as India-ink and there was otherwise not a sign of facial hair. She was of dark-brown complexion with a figure that brought to mind the mythological Greeks. Her breasts were bulging with a hint of her big, dark, pointed nipples protruding as if to challenge the passerby to stop, look, and wonder if anyone could surpass them. Her legs were stretched long and somewhat wide, while the rest of her body slid down the chair with her head over the backrest. Her arms seemed to have taken the opportunity to allow her luscious body do its thing as its owner decided to take refuge in deep sleep. Most probably in an awake state she would have had both her hands across her bosom to protect her from unwanted stares and intrusions into her privacy. Her clothes did indicate that she was well aware of her figure and had tried to downplay it. She was wearing a loose lavender turtleneck sweater and baggy jeans as travel clothes.

Robert, I mean Bob, was so engrossed in the lavish bodily splendor that he was chewing on his tobacco pipe as hard as he could and it cracked and caught his tongue in the crevice. This not only brought him back to reality but cut his tongue as well. He cursed. "Oh. Shi…SHOOOT!"

At least he had manners in mixed company. His real name was Robert Louis Stevenson. He did not write *Treasure Island*, but he did want to write a big blockbuster like that. Who doesn't want to? He was a writer and producer—to be precise he made movies. He wanted one of his movies to one day be a game changer and was currently producing a new one: *Kanishka*. The story was about an Indian immigrant living in Cleveland. Bob was using this as an excuse to just stand there and stare at this Indian-looking lady.

The commotion with the pipe disturbed the woman's nap. When she realized she'd unconsciously been posing like a life model for a painter, and that in the place of her painter was a tall, gruff-looking English chap, she was kind of disappointed and gave him one of those stern Gandhian looks, which spoke volumes.

Bob figured that he'd been caught red-handed. He had to make amends. He was a decent American living in a lakeside mansion on the outskirts of New York City. It was a ten-acre lot with large, grown trees and a well-manicured garden featuring precisely selected flowering bushes, all perennials, and sequenced to flower from the spring throughout the fall with different color combinations. The credit went to his wife, Betty. Betty was a good strong Democrat. She believed in volunteering for every cause that helped humanity. She felt that it was a solemn duty for every individual to take care of the under-privileged. Bob, though, was a staunch Republican and felt everyone should do their best to prosper on their own. He believed that handouts made people lazy and prompted bumming for everything, and that as the days went by they would start to consider it as their God-given right. This prompted Sam and Suzie, his children, to tend the garden with their mother in order to get a wage equivalent to their weekly allowance. Sam wanted to be a lawyer while Suzie intended to be a doctor. They took after their mom and dad respectively. Right now, Betty and the kids were off to the United Kingdom on a vacation.

Bob's mind was stuck as how to mend the situation with the woman he'd been staring at. *Honesty is the best policy*, he thought, and with a warm smile as he moved closer, he said, "My name is Robert Louis Stevenson."

"Yeah, my name is Catherine the Great, wife of Louis the fourteenth."

"Honestly it is."

With an innocent facial expression as if she'd never lie even if her life depended on it, the lady countered with a smile. "Honestly, so is mine."

Bob was taken aback for the first time in his life. She had a very charming accent, which let the listener know that English was not her native tongue. Her grooming, straight white teeth, scant make-up just where it was required, and God-given body did him in. For a second he even forgot he was married with two children. It is odd that society has made rules that restrict people from being themselves. If it had been up to Bob, he would have lifted this damsel up and taken her away to his cave even against her will. That's why we have developed rules of conduct.

She was smiling mischievously, as she was reading every thought that passed through his consciousness. Her figure had prompted many an encounter with unwanted solicitors. This had trained her sixth sense to decode every stray thought someone had for her.

Bob suddenly realized that she must have the capacity to decipher thoughts. Now not only had he got to think on his feet but he had also to clean his thoughts with a strong laundry detergent. "Scout's honor, I am Robert Stevenson; I write under the pseudonym Woodburn. Maybe you…heard…about…"

"You are the author from New York who was interviewed by Global Television Network, about your forthcoming movie, *Kanishka*."

She pronounced Kanishka with such purity that Bob realized she was from India. He'd always felt an affinity for people from the sub-continent…

for their intrinsic values and philosophy that has answers for all the questions of life and above all for the magnanimity of being able to comprehend and understand others' points of view. Most of his mental jigsaw puzzles were all answered by Indian philosophy. It became clear why this lady was his match for wit.

Having been vindicated by the sheer luck of appearing on Global, Bob replied in a confident assertive voice, "Yes I am he."

She read Bob's thoughts once again; she was not going to let him go. "You are taking advantage of a poor husband's story and sorrow to make quick cool million with your movie aren't you?"

This charge came on like a crouching tigress pouncing on a helpless deer. Bob felt like Jim Courbet, confronting the man-eater of Kaumon. When a tiger is hurt and has a hard time getting its prey, it finds a weak link, a local village girl or a boy to pounce upon to make a meal out of them. Humans are the weakest of all living creatures. There are at least few hundred billion living things on earth. Humans probably only constitute less than one-tenth of one percent, at least let me say so lest my only readers, the humans, throw this book out of the window. Bob was the weak link and the prowl was on by this lass with a body that resembled that of the big cat, the tiger.

Defensively, Bob countered, "No!"

"An Oscar maybe," she growled.

"No, it's not just a fictional movie. I call it a Docu-Fiction."

"You guys in movie-making always have names to burn."

"You are wrong again." Bob was trying very hard not to accept defeat. "It is a movie in the form of Docu-Fiction, hard hitting the senseless."

She cut him off abruptly... "The under-privileged who are fighting for a cause, which they are convinced is right," she said with a pause, smiling very mischievously. "I guess you are a staunch Republican aren't you?"

"Well I am a kind of... liberal Republican," he said warily.

"They all claim that," she said, picking up her bags. "No Republican can help that." She eyed the final boarding process to London, and continued. "Democrats have two big problems. One, they love people and want to do good to them collectively and they also really; really...*love* people, but individually on a one on one. Of course, Republicans only talk about it and splash it on the internet, while secretly carrying on with the secretary discreetly...Newt style."

Bob was being bombarded. In one non-offensive sentence she had expounded on love Clinton-style, as well as Newt-style. What was she? Republican or Democrat? She was quick on her feet and quite smart; her IQ must be high. As he gathered his thoughts, she was looking at the gate agent.

"We still have to get the count from the plane," she said. "It shouldn't be too long. I should make it."

"You're heading to London?" he said, trying to change the subject.

"You are changing the subject...uncomfortable aren't you?"

"Well...not exactly..."

"OK. I am heading off for a vacation to my homeland, India...and will be back in early September in time for school."

Seeing his puzzled look, she said, "I am a lawyer; I teach at Columbia."

"I teach at Columbia myself."

"I know you teach there too; your office is in the clouds. It overlooks the Liberty statue and you can see Ellis Island also. I know all about you and am a fan of your movies."

"Then."

"I wanted to give you some of your own treatment, always putting people on the defensive. I mean in your movies."

"Ms. K. Rao," came the announcement over the speaker.

"Catherine with a 'K,' is that it?"

"Wrong again. Kathyayani, but for people like you, Katherine with a K like...Kate Hepburn."

"I see."

"Got to go...Bye...find another innocent girl."

"What do you mean?"

Smirking as if she'd conquered and tamed the bull, she waltzed to the counter and picked-up her ticket and boarding pass. As she was entering the jetway she said, "I will meet your family on the flight. I will tell them what you have been doing here all this time."

"What was I doing?"

She walked away with a mischievous smile as if she knew what was going on in his mind. The female gender has been given an intuition to decipher what goes on in the minds of males, especially husbands.

He did not know what to expect. What was she up to? *She seems to know everything about me,* he thought. *What I do, where I work, and maybe where I live? Was she really asleep or was she faking it? Did she trick me?* His paranoia hit him. He started questioning everything she'd said and done in that short span of ten minutes. Notoriety gives you a lot of freedom. However, celebrity gives you absolutely no shelter from exposure and the ills that follow. He suddenly remembered the movie *Fatal Attraction.* It sent a chill through his spine. A similar chill is called bliss in Hindu philosophy. With a name like Kathyayani, she was a Hindu. Kathyayani was the name of the god mother, Lalitha. She was not, absolutely not someone who would take advantage of a minor aberration in a man's mind. Bob did have to be truthful with himself. You can lie to the whole world, but you have to be truthful to your conscience.

Bob's wild imagination usually took over and kept him straight always. He always wanted to be all the characters he had created. The last short story he had written was about a palmist who predicted his own death.

Bob's clarity of thought in managing the sequence of the events and the character development in films were the mainstays of his meteoric rise to fame in the closely guarded movie field of New York. He had his office on one of the top floors looking out onto the Hudson. Every time he looked at Ellis Island, he remembered his dad and mom.

His dad had come to New York in the late sixties. He always claimed that he was following an American Dream. As his days were coming to an end, he often mentioned his American Dream had been shattered within two decades of his arrival in America. He said that the cause was the Republican ideology of promoting individual investors to develop small to medium industries and later turn them into big corporations. Their motivation was always to increase the wealth of the corporation. His claim to fame was an owner-run company that always took care of their employees, because they knew that the employees were the wealth generators. They took care of their benefactors. Whereas the corporations are soul-less, pleasing the stock holders, and not the stake holders.

He said that all the MBAs from the big universities only thought to number crunch. Their aim was to get the analyzers to over-valuate the stock price. This is a manipulation game. It's the biggest con game of the twenty-first century. He had his own version of an award, the Moron Award. It was always awarded to the CEO who closed a plant to improve profits by fifteen-million dollars, to quench the thirst of the Wall Street moguls, while awarding himself a bonus of sixty-million dollars, which was what the plant's gross was, with forty-five million for expenses.

He believed that the Republicans should go back to helping the owner-operated industry and give the corporate giants a kick in the ass, since they deserved it. As you can see, he had a simplistic view of the world. However, with the Enron case, and other fiascos, it may be that his view is simplistic but has merit.

His idea was that Harvard, Yale, and Princeton should impart more wisdom and not simply teach manipulation of figures.

That may be the reason Bob was a Republican but was finding it hard to get his father's views across to the big guys. So he took to making movies on the shattered American Dream. As he was slowly walking out of the terminal, he heard a shrill shout, "Mr. Stevenson."

He turned around and saw a pretty damsel in a United uniform running out from the United Airlines ticket counter. The airlines do make their uniforms more or less like body wraps. They accentuate the obvious and the employees also make themselves over in a very attractive way. Mr. Stevenson Sr. always used to say that when the first commercial flights started there was not a man who did not get infatuated with the stewardess on the flight. He used to joke that the stewardesses had to have a fly swatter to keep the men away. Bob's older sister had been offered a position as a stewardess, but Senior did not allow her to take the position.

"Yes?" said Bob.

These movie guys can make things happen. They make a pure yes into a question. Bob had a unique way of writing. His conversational dialogue always had an interjecting style. Timing was key for an artist to get the maximum out of his lines. A few seconds' delay in the rendering kills the impact and ruins the flow of the movie. It was always a challenge for the artists. Bob hated melodrama. Recently he had started to dabble in moralistic movie productions. He had been interviewed on the Global Television Network in that regard. That was what Miss K had been referring to.

"I love all your movies and writing," said the young woman in the United uniform.

"Hum," was all he could mutter. He was pre-occupied by the jolt the young lawyer had given him, and was still contemplating what she meant by "tell" his wife. He didn't care. However, he was curious. He'd had his few flings with his starlets but never anything serious. His wife always said anyone who could put up with his wild imagination as well as his mood swings could have him with her blessings. He was a popular boy right now after the Global interview.

The young woman handed him a copy of "The Palmist." "May I have you autograph this copy please?"

He quickly signed the copy and got on his way. Usually they follow it up with "May I come and see you? I am an artist looking for a break. I am willing to put in long hours. I will do anything to get a break." This usually becomes their downfall. The guys take this literally and you know what happens. The men get to do everything but the young women do not get the break. Every coffee shop, every bar, every restaurant, every convenience store, and every which way you look, you will find a young, pretty girl who has been trapped in this masquerade. They often tell their families that they are on the verge of a big role.

As Bob got out, he flagged a JFK Flyer and the driver recognized him and stopped. Bob got on the bus. As the bus sped away from JFK, Bob saw the United flight taking off into a clear blue sky with some scattered clouds. When one sees the sky they should really enjoy the warmth of the universal colors: the blue, the white clouds, and the lingering reddish hue of the dawn. It is said the Hindus believe that the skin color of Vishnu the creator is a soft, sky-blue color. Its significance is to let people know that the Lord is as vast as the universe itself. Bob reflected to himself aloud, "What a powerful concept of the Lord."

"Did you say something, Mr. Stevenson?" the driver asked.

"No, nothing important."

That's what is wrong with the world right now. The concept of God is not important. What is God anyway? Isn't he a figment of human imagination?

If we believe that he is omnipotent, omniscient, and omnipresent, then what are we? If I call myself as an individual entity separate from God, then he has lost his trait of being omnipresent. That means God is in me. Better still, I am God. If we believe that God is restricted to one specific group of people, say the followers of Islam, then he has lost his trait of being omnipresent. Omniscient—let's not explore that issue; all our dirty thoughts will spill over. However, we can keep no secrets from him.

Job description of God, what is it? The JFK Flyer reached the subway station and Bob got off and took the train to Manhattan.

Chapter Three

Third week in August 2001

Bob emerged on the corner of Hudson Street and West Broadway. The New York morning crowd was just getting started. He went to the familiar paper vendor at the corner, picked up the morning paper, and looked at the main headlines. Mid-east unrest, Irish conflict, Indo-Pak skirmish, trouble in Philippines, and FLQ in the so-called peace-loving Canada. As if there was nothing new, he folded the paper and held it under his left armpit as he filled his pipe with tobacco and lit it. He smoked a very expensive blend with an aroma that drove people crazy. It was like the commercial for the after-shave, Hai-Karate. As he started to puff on his pipe, many a passerby inhaled and paid attention to him and his aromatic second-hand smoke.

The ferry from Staten Island was chugging slowly to the New York side of the Hudson. The breeze was gently blowing from the northeast direction. There stood on the deck a pretty brunette. She was only five feet and an inch tall. Her face was a rectangular mold. Long hair was fluttering in the breeze. She wore an expensive pair of sunglasses and had accentuated high cheekbones, which were highlighted with very exacting Max Factor product. Her lips were just right—not too lush, but neither too small, with a bright-red lipstick. She wore a purple dress draping her right down to her knees, with a shoe color that matched not her dress but the scarf she was sporting. She was clearly very confident in herself and was carrying a briefcase made of the softer kind of rich leather. Her briefcase had a tag, which revealed her business card. She was, as the card suggested, Ms. Priya, along with a last name too long to even to dare to mention. She worked for RLS Productions as the associate producer/director. Priya was contemplating something when her thoughts were interrupted by:

"Hey Priya, I was looking for you all over."

"Hi Monisha."

"What are you looking at? Your grand office over-looking the Hudson?"

"What's that all about?" asked Priya.

"I was talking to one of your so-called cousins."

"Oh no."

"He was pissed that you had an office that over-looked the Statue of Liberty."

"And?"

"He has his in that dingy Wall Street building."

"Where did you meet him?"

"In the bar last night."

"Didn't he have anything better to do?"

"Obviously not. He tried to hit on me. So crude. When he found out that I was waiting for you, he scrammed from there. What happened? You left me hanging in there all by myself."

"I had to read a script, one of those experimental screenplay guys."

"What did you think?"

"Quite interesting I just read the beginning. He is going to give his pitch."

"Coming from you, it must be good."

A big thud meant that the ferry had docked and it was time to get off with everyone else. The women looked like two Hollywood starlets disembarking from an ocean liner. In the movie *How to Marry a Millionaire,* three girls get off an ocean liner in a quest for millionaires. However, these two didn't need millionaire boyfriends or hubbies. Priya, in her own right, was an actress, with at least five type-cast roles the likes of Maria in *West Side Story,* Fiona in *Brigadoon,* etc, before becoming producer/director, while Monisha, with her criminal law practice, was hitting close to becoming a millionaire anyway. Many a man who was standing by was watching them with an admiring look, hoping for a chance to date either of them.

"I've got to go; Bob must have been waiting for me."

"Are we getting together this evening?"

"Yes, make it a little later, say seven-thirty."

"OK."

Priya hurried down the crosswalk to hit Chambers Street and started to walk down Chambers. Chambers starts at the corner of Hudson and West Broadway. That is a peculiar, five-street junction. West Broadway and Hudson cross each other and Chambers, then jet off at a forty-five-degree angle heading northeast. On the southwest corner stands a Starbucks coffee shop. It was customary for Priya and Bob to have a coffee in the morning and review their schedules for the day. This was their morning kick-off meeting, so to speak. Chambers Street was a blue-collar area and Priya usually got at least five to ten whistles. She kept a count on the number each day. It gave her an upper hand over the male species. She was walking at a fast pace but not too fast, in order to avoid perspiring.

She maintained herself in a fresh-as-a-daisy state throughout the day and late into the evening. A lot of people wondered how she did it. She prided herself on her looks and how she maintained herself. Her clothes were custom made. She often designed and embroidered her clothes herself. Her genes must have taught her those traits. It was said she was once a Miss-Something but she never talked about it. As she was getting close to the five-street junction, she spotted Bob leaning on a light-post and smoking away on his pipe.

She had abruptly stopped at the crossing because of a red crossing signal. Usually New Yorkers don't pay any attention to signals. She waved to Bob. He waved back and watched her wait for the light to change. Since the lights had to negotiate five streets of traffic it usually took a while to get your turn. Bob looked at her and suddenly he remembered Ms. K. There were a lot of similarities between Priya and her. Ms. K had a more sculpted body build, while Priya was petite and more a Pretty Young Thing.

The signal changed and Priya crossed the road and met up with Bob.

"So the family is off on their European vacation?" she said.

"Yep."

Bob was still pondering on the girl he'd met at the airport. Priya always read his mind well and felt he was in his private space. She let him stay there and left him to his thoughts as they walked down towards the Starbucks. Bob, still maintaining the silence and puffing his pipe, sat at their regular table on the outside.

KANISHKA

Priya waltzed inside to find there were at least five customers before her. A Patel family who had come to this country as refugees from Uganda ran the coffee shop. Priya was a second-generation U.S. citizen but the Patel family identified her as their own kith and kin. She had that kind of effect on people she met. She talked in a soft but firm voice and made people feel important. She did not come across as someone who was high handed, but soft pedaling. Her dad had come as an immigrant to Canada. He always reminded his children about how he'd come and what had transpired in the first twenty-four hours of his immigrant life, when he'd had a meagre sixteen Canadian dollars. Priya recalled the story very well.

"*Priya, bittiya tumhare coffee thayar hai aakey lejaye yey,*" Tanvi said in Hindi.[1]

Mrs. Tanvi Patel wanted her son to marry a professional girl like Priya. She always served Priya and Bob their orders herself. It was a privilege Priya had because she was from the same mother country.

"Thank you, Aunty." Priya paid the bill with a ten for an eight-dollar charge and picked up the coffee and waltzed back to Bob, who was sitting outside. The late-August weather felt like fall, chilly but not unbearable.

Priya placed the coffee on the table and sat across from Bob, who was still in his thoughts. "Something bothering you?" she asked.

"No, nothing at all. I just met a Kat."

"Big-bosomed brunette, I suppose."

There was silence from Bob as if he knew that Priya could read his mind. Priya did read his mind and left his thoughts to his own private space. She continued to sip on her latte.

"What's up today?" he finally asked.

"That guy with that one-man show or screenplay or what not...*Kanishka.*"

After a pause, he responded, "PG. Isn't he the one we met in 1988?"

"Yes, we felt let down because he went AWOL."

"*Kanishka* was not a good name then and it's not a good name now. Doesn't have an American ring to it."

Priya was pissed to hear that comment. "Why? Is it too Indian for your American brain? You are all descended from the guy who didn't know where he was and called the native people Indians. Co-lum-bus. And after finding

---

1 "Priya, your coffee is ready. Come and get it. You are like my daughter."

out the truth, you guys continued calling them not white Indians but red Indians, so you could maintain white superiority…and you call *Kanishka* not a good name? Kanishka was an emperor from the Gupta Empire and Mourya Dynasty. He was a Buddhist and preached non-violence."

"You made your point."

"So did you."

"What about PG?" asked Bob.

Priya and Bob had these kinds of tiffs all the time. Both enjoyed them.

"He is coming today at eleven a.m." she answered.

"With what?"

"A rewritten version from his one-man-show concept."

He sipped his coffee. "Did he apologize for going AWOL?"

"No. But he said after we hear him out we will know why he did. He claims that he has a script in the form of a scenario, more along the lines of a movie."

"Hope he doesn't bore us with his directorial capacities," grumped Bob.

"He was very crisp on the phone and shows a lot of promise," said Priya.

"Do you want to direct this project?"

"I would like to. It's up my alley…about an Indian family."

"Now back to Kanishka." said Bob.

"Are you bribing me with the previous comment?"

"No, not at all. But *Kanishka* doesn't do it." said Bob. "Not a marketable name."

"Right on. How about *Anguish*?"

Bob always started with the marketing side of the product. He said the hype in the early stages drove the box office. "We need to employ all our marketing strategies to sell the product and make a killing in the first few weeks," was his motto. His main strategy was to make the movie with minimum cash out but create a class product. He always called his films "products."

"Anguish…hum…A N G U I S H…there is a ring to it," he mused.

Bob began his projects by creating the poster. His poster then guided him to the final product. He always maintained that it was the ads that always attracted the audience. He'd won the best poster awards at least four times in the last five years. His designs constituted the break-even for the office he maintained on the eighty-first floor overlooking the Hudson.

"Alright, *Anguish*. I can buy that." Priya said, as she finished her latte.

Bob asked Priya to go ahead and said he would follow her in an hour or so.

Priya walked down the street westward and came to the imposing office building. As she was climbing the front steps, everyone greeted her. She was very popular. She entered through the revolving doors and walked towards the elevators. She got into the elevator and was pushed to the back.

"Good morning, good looking," said a bloke from a neighboring office as he pressed their floor on the elevator.

The elevator started to speed up. On the way up it was always smooth but when it came down, everyone's stomachs got a queer feeling. That was par for the course. Go up in style but come down with a thump. Guess it's life.

As the elevator slowed and then stopped, Priya got out of the elevator and followed the corridor to the back of the floor where there were big, double-glass doors. There was an artistic sign on the doors. "R. L. Stevenson Productions - One Movie at a Time." Priya walked in and greeted the receptionist, whose name was Simrin.

"Good morning."

"Good morning, Priya."

"What's on the schedule?"

"Your meeting at eleven with PG Woodward."

"Did you arrange lunch to be brought in?"

"Yes, and you have coffee and some soft drinks."

"Can you have the video recording started at eleven?"

"Will do."

At RLS they always recorded their meetings so as not to miss any important details. This was a very important meeting.

For some reason there was an unknown force that was guiding them through this particular meeting. Psychic persuasion, divine intervention, or maybe the power of love.

Everyone in the office was feeling somewhat uneasy about the meeting. They all knew this weird guy from Cleveland and wanted to help him. They had been kind of disappointed in their last encounter with him. He'd come up with this incredible storyline, but after everyone had gotten excited about it, he'd gone AWOL on them.

Priya was new with the production company. She had just graduated with an MFA from the University of Wisconsin, Madison Campus. Bob was a close friend of her dad's and it had opened the door for her. As it always happens, her dad had this friend in Cleveland who recommended PG to him, and he in turn, instead of recommending him directly to Bob, had asked Priya to handle it. Priya was kind of blunt with her dad and asked him to do his own recommendations. But her dad always had answers for everything. He said that favors he asked from people were always to help his kids only and that he wouldn't want to waste his balance in Bob's emotional bank account. So, for the second time, Priya was forced to recommend PG's story and proposal for a movie screenplay, much against the normal practices of the industry.

"Let him explain his trials and tribulations. Be patient, Beti, he has endured a lot of grief and has had to come to the stage of acceptance," urged her dad. Her dad even followed up on his recommendation to Bob as well. They were good friends.

Chapter Four

July 21st, 1970

Mr. Peter Gustav Smith was his name. He responded to PG, but he liked to be called Mr. Woodward—that is, PG Woodward. He'd always felt that Smith was too common a name. His wife Julia said that so was Woodward. She claimed Woodward was plastered all over the town. In the eighties there had been a small department store named Woodward. Every town had one on the main street. One need not ask for directions to Woodward. Just head off to Main Street, Any Town, and there stood a Woodward. Julia kidded him that Woodward was no better than Smith. Both were common names.

PG disagreed, while knowing the real truth behind his motivation. His favorite novel was *Damsel in Distress*, by PG Wodehouse. He had a crush on the heroine of the novel. She was wealthy and beautiful. She sported straight white teeth, unlike others from the good old country. The character liked tennis and one of its stars. She fantasized about meeting this bloke under the bleachers at Wimbledon and making passionate love. PG was a dreamer. He wanted to be the creator of this fantasy. But his drinking buddy at the local bar in Cleveland had worried him about using Wodehouse as his pen name. The friend said that the Brits might sue him for using their writer's name. So PG picked a Canadian department store's name instead.

Julia and their two children loved PG because he was a purist. He was simple, unassuming, and uncomplicated. He never had an ulterior motive for anything. Very loving. His wild imagination was a pleasant diversion for the whole family. When the children had been young, he used to tell them stories of concocted villains and princesses in the la la land of Arabia. It was his version of the *Arabian Nights*.

The story goes that there was an Arabian king who married and had his wife tell him stories. If she could not keep the stories coming, she would be beheaded the next day. This wife started telling him a long, drawn-out story that came to a cliffhanger by early dawn. The king had to let her live to know the end. She continued that way every night. These were the *Arabian Nights* stories. PG had his version of *Cleveland Northern Lights* stories. He used to take his family to a state park on Lake Erie, pitch a tent, and look toward the Canadian sky in the north. If they were lucky and if Mother Nature permitted, the sky would light up with Aurora Borealis. He used to have his son on one side and his daughter on the other, and he told them that this was God's IMAX Theater. The colors changed; they flowed like a curtain fluttering in a cool, gentle breeze. There were mixtures of colors in hues of red, blue, and white. "Is even nature scared of America's might?" he used to ask them.

He liked to frequent a local bar that he called The Pub Locale. He often went there and pretended that he was in the UK. He'd met Julia when he was in England on a work-related trip and had taken an excursion to Stratford. He'd wanted to see where that guy Shakespeare was born and where he'd written all that literature with that funny English. There was a theater there, where they were playing *The Merchant of Venice*. He saw the matinee, and afterwards he sat in a nearby restaurant facing a lake or a river. Julia was a waitress at the place. She ignored PG because he was staring at her. In England, because they live on a small island 300 miles wide and some 450 miles long, forgetting about Scotland and Ireland, of course, they like their privacy. They don't like eye contact. It makes them feel invaded. In America, if we don't make eye contact we think someone is hiding something. Julia was self-conscious. She told her co-host that there was this Yankee staring at her. The co-host eyed him and pronounced him a good catch. What next?

As Julia was taking an order at a table some ways away, Julia's friend approached PG in order to take his order.

PG said, "Thou shall telleth Portia to come and serveth me."

"What the hell are you talking?"

PG came down to earth with that rebuke. "I want Portia to serve me."

"Portia who?"

PG pointed towards Julia.

"Her name is Julia, not Portia."

"She looks just like Portia in the play I just saw. So for me she is Portia."

"OK, I will send her." She went into the kitchen, and so did Julia, to find out the scoop.

"He is smitten by you; he thinks you look like that girl who plays Portia."

"Really? He thinks I look like her? She is the most beautiful star in Shakespearian theater, and he thinks I look like her?"

She was, as they say in cricket, clean bowled. She powdered her nose, straightened her dress, propped up her boobs, and straightened her blond hair. As she was about to go, her friend gave her a thumbs up.

"You are a real friend, what should I do?"

"Say yes to whatever it is. We will worry later."

"OK. Wish me luck."

"Land him on the moon, baby. Land him on the moon."

"I will, yes I will." Julia headed out of the kitchen towards PG's table.

PG, meanwhile, was wondering what to say if she came. Should he ask her for a date? Should he ask her for her name? Silly, he already knew her name. Suddenly he became very nervous. He started reliving the play. What did Bassanio do? What did Antonio advise Bassanio? How did he approach Portia?

He was fumbling like a football quarterback. The British have this quaint way of setting their tables. On his table was a napkin with a pewter ring holding it. PG got hold of it in his hand. As Julia was approaching the table, he saw her and imagined her wearing Portia's costume and himself in Bassanio's clothes. As she was coming closer, his heart started beating hard and his pulse rate rose. She looked like an angel in a white, fluffy dress. Really she was wearing a drab-brown restaurant uniform, with stains from serving food. A mixture of strawberry, blueberry, and mustard colors were on the apron covering her brown dress.

The whole kitchen staff was out in the main restaurant in anticipation of some fireworks. The commotion got all the patrons interested in the happenings at that table too. The last time a bloke had tried to ask Julia out, he'd had his teeth out with the slap she had given him. Quickly, the kitchen staff laid bets on what was going to ensue. "Ten to one she will slap him." said one as he took the bets.

Her friend who knew her said, "Ten to ten she will go out with him."

An old lady from London said she hoped that they would marry and live happily for a long time.

Minutes were long, and seemed like hours. A Scottish party pooper interrupted Julia's advance by requesting a glass of water. One of the other staff volunteered to serve him.

Julia was about ten feet from the table where PG was shivering and worrying about what was going to happen. One thing going for him was his compliment to her, saying she looked like the actress who played the role of Portia.

Ten, nine, eight, seven, six, five, four, three, two-----------blastoff.

Julia stood just in front of him and looked at him. PG was not able to utter a word. They stared into each other's eyes. Eyes have the tendency to not hide any emotions. They are probably the best lie-detector tools. Suddenly, PG dropped on his knees as he grabbed on to her right hand. This was not something those who were witnessing the drama had expected.

Slowly but firmly PG stuttered, "Oh, my dearest Portia, will thou marry me, here and right now? You are my angel and I am smitten by you and cannot live my life without you anymore."

Julia was not used to anything like this. Everyone who hit on her usually wanted a date and a one-night stand. She did go on dates but had never lost her virginity. This twist was something she was not ready for. But their eyes did not lie; both had some kind of feeling about each other and it was positive.

The old lady turned to Mr. Jeeves, who was holding the bets, and she announced herself as the winner.

Julia did not say a word, but did not take her hand away from PG. He took it as an acceptance and quickly slipped the pewter ring onto her finger. She dropped down on her knees to his level, and they both looked at each other. The rest was history. They kissed, they married, and they produced one of each: Rose and Abe.

Chapter Five

Third week of August 2001.

PG got off the train at New York's Grand Central Station. The Amtrak train had come all the way from Chicago via Cleveland and Albany. PG had stopped flying twelve years before and had started using Amtrak always. It didn't matter if the trains were late; they were, according to him, safer. He left Grand Central, hailed a cab, and asked the driver to take him to the corner of Wall Street and Broadway. He got out, paid the driver, and went into a building on Wall Street. A few minutes later he came out shaking his head. Suddenly, the taxi driver showed up with a briefcase and a portfolio. PG thanked him and took his belongings. He started looking around for a public phone booth. There was one in the corner. He put in some coins and dialed 212-911-2001.

"Good morning. Stevenson Productions, may I help you?"
"This is PG and I have an appointment with Priya at eleven."
"Mr. Woodward, she is expecting you, sir."
"I'm at the corner of Wall Street and Broadway."
"We moved to this location over three years ago, sir."
"How do I get there?"
"Just follow Broadway west all the way to the City Hall area."
"Broadway west all the way?"
"It opens into a wide-open space past Chambers and Hudson."
"Just a minute. I'm writing down Chambers and Hudson."
"You will see two office buildings and we are in the second building."

"Second building."

"Suite 81111."

"Eight-one-one-one-one."

"It shouldn't take too long to get here."

"See you guys in a while." He collected his belongings and started walking westward, at a hasty pace.

Soon, the elevator doors on the eighty-first floor opened. Out came PG with his belongings. He was shabbily dressed and wearing a pair of slippers. His name should have been PJ instead of PG. His pants were like PJs. His hair was not properly combed. He looked like someone with a mission to accomplish. His face looked like it had been carved in stone. His demeanor was somber and he looked like a rock beaten up by the insistent waves from the ocean. There was a very lonely feeling surrounding him.

He walked through the corridor to the back of the building and saw the impressive double-door entrance of Stevenson Productions.

The glass doors opened and PG entered as Simrin was going through a Macy's catalog. She looked up and glanced at PG. Simrin was a very attractive girl. She had a round face adorned with black-rimmed spectacles, which looked as if someone older had chosen them. She had a complexion that would have put her at the top of the list as a model for Max Factor. Her smile was pleasant and her voice was sweet. "So you had no problems finding us, Mr. Woodward?"

"Your directions were just right."

"Priya is on a long-distance call, but I will let her know you are here. Please take a seat. May I bring you a Diet Coke?"

"How did you know that I drink Diet Coke?"

"It's our duty to learn all the likes and dislikes of our customers, and to please them at all costs."

"I once knew a waitress who was like that…I miss her."

PG had tears in his eyes. Simrin, in her haste to fetch him the Coke, missed it as she went into the main conference room. There in one corner was Bob with his poster. On the bottom third of the poster was *Anguish* plastered with two-inch brush strokes in bright, blood red. In the background was the Sanskrit word OM. It was in bright yellow with a dark-blue border. The background of the poster was a pure green. It was an attractive advertisement that would create interest in learning more. That was Bob's strength. Priya's strength was to direct the technical aspects of the movie. This was the first time Bob was considering letting Priya direct a movie alone with complete creative freedom.

"Sorry, didn't mean to disturb you," said Simrin. "Just getting a Coke"
"Did PG show up?"
"Yes, I am waiting for Priya to finish her call with the Dream Team."
"OK."
"May I get you a coffee?"
"Hum."

That meant yes. Simrin poured a coffee from the flask into a mug and served it to him, and took the Diet Coke for PG from the refrigerator. Back in the reception area, as she was handing PG the can, she noticed that in that chiseled face of his there was wetness.

"Is there something bothering you?" she asked.
"No, only memories. Memories of my last visit here."
"When was that?"
"Close to twelve years ago."
"That long ago and you still remember."
"There are some things that you can never forget. They are usually two kinds. One which brings happiness and other which brings grief."
"I don't remember anything from the past. Maybe I have a bad memory."
"You are lucky. It means you have had a very happy, un-eventful past."
Priya arrived and butted in. "Hi. PG. How are you?"
Short and sweet was the answer. "I'm OK."
"Shall we go to the main conference room?"
"You're the boss. Whatever."
"Simrin, will you please get me a coffee and a Diet Coke for PG."
"I already have one," he said. "But thanks."
Priya smiled at the receptionist. "Simrin, we want you to join in this meeting. This would be start of your promotion to associate director."
Simrin didn't know what to say, so she said "You're the boss. Whatever."
She thought it was cool.

The three of them entered the conference room. Out of the window they saw the Newark airport flights taking off and the Statue of Liberty standing majestically. Suddenly, the expression on PG's face changed as if a dark cloud had moved over him. He stared at the view, rubbing his eyes with the sleeve of his shirt. His expression changed again, and in a firm, strong voice, he said, "Shut the blinds on the window, please. I don't need to see out."

Bob was immediately offended. He prided himself on his conference room and the view. He didn't see any reason for them to close the blinds. Priya knew what was happening between the two. The author lives his script himself while the producer is pragmatic and doesn't understand the author's likes and dislikes.

Simrin came to the rescue. "Some people have memories of the last visit and so they prefer…" She suddenly found herself in a bad spot and didn't know how to get out of it. "…closed blinds," she finished, as she closed the blinds of the panoramic window.

Bob wanted to have the last word on this situation. "Yes I have memories of someone going AWOL on me."

PG's face went red and his expression turned hostile. He looked at Priya suspiciously, as if she had neglected to mention something to Bob. Then he exploded.

"You son of a bitch, I said that by the end of this session, you would get to it, but you with your bloated ego cannot be patient. You're a writer, aren't you? Shame on you, for playing with human frailties. Understanding is what you need. you goddamn big shot."

Bob hadn't expected this outburst, and Priya didn't know how to salvage the situation. But Simrin sometimes came up with dandy little sayings, and now she provided one. "My grandmother always said that memories and scars always go together. Happy memories are often forgotten quickly. The scared ones stay with you and the only unstoppable entity in the universe is time, which has the capacity to heal. Maybe we all might have to wait for the right time."

This gave Priya a chance to jump in. "Bob, let's give this a reasonable chance to take its own shape without trying to architect outcomes, and vent frustrations. I know why you're angry but let's hear it out. We may all end up on the same page again."

When on the defensive, Bob never got very angry with anyone. He had a tendency to put other people on the defense. That was a way he got them to think on their feet and not put their mouths in gear before their minds. He had always been very adept psychologically as regarded people and their problems. He felt that people who did not avail themselves of a window of opportunity always lost out in the end. In his opinion, PG was one of these people. It's very difficult to apologize to someone who has called you a son of a bitch, but Bob showed his mettle. "PG, I'm sorry. It was insensitive of me to put you on the spot, before you had your chance to speak."

The anger and outrage in PG disappeared, and the six-foot, two-hundred-pound hulk of a man started to sob. Then he sobbing turned to weeping. Priya, Bob, and Simrin were all stunned.

PG's weeping turned into literally crying like a baby. Tears flowed from his eyes and he was just out of control. A man does not cry unless he is carrying a big burden.

Simrin got out of her seat, went to him, and started to comfort him. He hugged her and continued to cry. Simrin gave him her dupatta.[2]

"Why don't you take five?" she said to the others. "I'll stay with him."

Bob and Priya left the room. The crying continued on Simrin's shoulders.

"I will get to it, I will get to it eventually," PG sobbed.

"Yes PG, you can get to it whenever you want."

"I'm glad you understand."

Overhearing the conversation, Bob and Priya wondered. Meanwhile, Simrin was at a loss because she didn't know what it was he thought she understood.

The healing time passed and the crying slowly moved to weeping. Weeping went back to sobbing, and then PG said, "Call them in. We have to start and get going—we don't have time to waste."

Simrin moved back to her chair as Bob and Priya reentered and took their seats.

There was silence plastered all over the place. Everyone was waiting for the other to take the lead. PG sat with his eyes closed to try to get them back to normal. The other three were lost as to what to do. It looked as if PG was organizing his thought process. He opened his eyes, grabbed his portfolio, and pulled out a bunch of storyboard material. Each of the boards was numbered with Act, Scene, and Shot. PG sorted them out. "Bear with

---

2 A scarf or head covering

me, we'll start off with Act Two. This is a flashback and then come back to the sequence."

"Take your time, and present it the way you want. It's your creation, you have artistic freedom," Bob assured him.

Chapter Six

Third week of August 2001

The storyboard had an illustration of an airline counter. PG glanced at Priya and then made eye contact with Bob, followed by Simrin. His eyes spoke volumes when he looked at Simrin. She had won herself close friend and confidante status with him. He moved up to his storyboard, cleared his throat and started to put his creation into words. "It's Vancouver, Canada."

The storyboard had a caption, which said Act One—Scene Eight. PG stopped and put the board back into the pile. He pulled out a number of boards and placed them on the ledge of the white dry-eraser board. The eraser board was flanked with camera equipment on one side, and on the other was some editing equipment.

The three subjects were anxiously waiting. They didn't want to upset PG, lest he break down again.

The top board had a caption: Act Two—Scene One. PG cleared his throat again, looked at the three of them, and started again with feeling and in earnest. One could see that this was flowing from his heart. It is said that God gives every human being one whack at good artistic endeavor.

June 21st, 1985

The place was Cleveland. The street, Lakeside Drive was on the far east side of the city. This exclusive mansion setting had a unique wall around a certain compound. It looked like something that had come from old England. But it had been conceived by Mamta, who hailed from India. She was born in a village in the southern Indian state of Andhra Pradesh. The village was on an island called Bobbarlanka. The river Godavari, as it approaches the Bay of Bengal, opens up into six to seven sub-tributaries. These form the islands with locks to hold the river waters back. This area is called Konaseema. Mamta had grown up there with her grandparents. He was a collector, a big position during the British Raj. As he was privileged he could afford a big mansion. He had peons wearing cross belts with brass British emblems on them, giving them authority. It was from there Mamta had imported her ideas about the compound wall.

The entry was adorned with a double gate, remotely operated, with two brick pillars and pedestals. On the pedestals were two granite sculptures of squatting Bengal tigers. The driveway extended through thick maple trees into a big roundabout, with the left side opening up to a large parking area and a four-car garage with four individual doors. The main entry was a majestic double door. It opened up into a foyer with an interior fountain and a pond with water lilies and lotus flowers. When she was a child, Mamta had always played by a pond where there were lotus. Her home had a lot of coconut palms and flowering trees. Since she was now living in Cleveland, she had insisted that her architect consider a greenhouse in the main entrance along with this pond.

Mamta, as she was called, was always paged as Dr. Mamta Rao. She had a roaring practice at Cleveland General. She and her husband, Dr. Rohit Rao, a neuro-surgeon, had come to the United States in the early seventies, quickly completed the boards, and set up practice. Their earnest wish to help, their friendly demeanor, and their real, honest concern for their patients quickly got them the name of true humanitarians. A lot of other doctors wondered what their secret was. They wondered how the Raos did it. How was it they were so liked by all their patients? Their practice doubled and then tripled in the span of just a few years. If a patient walked through their door, that was it, they never wanted to leave and go to any other doctor.

One of the local priests commented that they were the personification of the "love thy neighbor as thyself" doctrine from the Bible. It is one of the most misinterpreted passages. The Good Samaritan was not a privileged individual, but he helped someone who did not belong to his own faith. The Raos claimed that in Hindu philosophy, (note, not religion but philosophy) it is said, *"Manawa Seve Madhava Seva."* This philosophy, initially imparted through word of mouth by the learned, (again, not priests) was later transcribed in Sanskrit onto palm leaves. *Manawa* means human and humanity. *Seva* means service. *Madhava* means lord. Another name for *Madhava* is *Govinda*. *Govinda* means destroyer of ignorance. It is believed in Hindu philosophy that every time you utter *Govinda*, one layer of ignorance is removed from your thought process. The Raos claimed that Hindu philosophy teaches what is the same as a true Christian way of life, and that they followed it.

Service to humanity is service to God.

If a patient came to their door without insurance, they didn't send him away. Instead, they checked him out and sent him to the local government-funded, county hospital. Their physician samples were always given to the underprivileged and those who could not afford to buy drugs. Unlike other doctors, their home telephone number was listed, and their patients were free to call them any time they wanted, even in the middle of the night.

One of their patients, a Mexican migrant worker, had a sick parent. This worker was poor and did odd jobs to keep his family going. He stumbled upon Mamta, who treated his father and gave him all his medical help for free. While she was treating his father, she noticed his mother favoring the right side of the body. She went on to give her a physical unasked and treated her too. This family considered Mamta an angel sent by God. The worker and his family now took care of the garden for the Raos. In turn, as if what they had done was not enough, the Raos let the family live in the cottage at the back of their house, facing Lake Erie. They didn't charge them rent. They even got the worker a large riding lawn mower and got him into business for himself. They pleaded with INS and got the family Green Cards. This is what is called going over and above the call of duty. This is probably what Jesus meant when he told the parable of The Good Samaritan.

It was an early morning in Cleveland. The rays of the sun had just peered into Mamta's bedroom. It was a large room with a king-size bed. The sheets were satin and Rohit was still in bed. Mamta got up and quickly waltzed into the bathroom. There was no one in the room, but she still was modest, covering her body with a white satin cover, which was transparent enough for the beholder to gasp at her beautiful, perfect figure. I am afraid to say anything more lest her divinity might place a curse on me. But this I have to mention. She saw her face in the mirror. The red mark on her forehead was all smudged and had spread onto her lush cheeks. She remembered the night before. Rohit didn't want her to leave him and go on a vacation. He had said he would miss her and the kids. She had kind of joked that he would be OK.

She looked at the smudge, which spoke volumes. She was glad she'd found it before her kids started to make fun of them. And it kind of put a smirk on her face as she proceeded to wash. She quickly jumped into the shower and started to shampoo her long hair, which draped down to her knees. It was thick and luxuriant. Her face was round with a very well carved forehead. Her eyebrows were thin and long and jet-black. Below them, two eyes that were like petals from a fully-grown lotus adorned them. The eyelashes were thick, well maintained, and also jet-black. The whites were pure and bright. The pupils were a kind of brownish black. Her nose was chiseled and looked like it was out of a Ravi Varma painting. Her lips and her mouth were attractive and very inviting. Often, people marveled that she had brains along with her stunning features. She was a bit plump in her body but her five-foot height more than compensated. As she walked out of the shower, her color was a wheatish white. Her body did not have one unwanted mark on it and neither were there any moles to speak off. Witnessing her long hair, one would have expected a lot of body hair, but she had a perfect body with absolutely none.

She quickly put on a robe, and after she had dried her hair, she placed a red dot on her forehead and left the bathroom. She opened the bedroom door and walked into the main foyer. The foyer was circular and had a decorative railing. One could see down into the family room and kitchen. On the front side were two semicircular steps leading to the ground floor.

The time was six in the morning. The automatic CD player was programmed to start playing early morning chants in praise of the creator. Mamta walked across to the kids' bedrooms and peeped into them. Both Seshi, her twenty-two year old daughter, who was in a med program, and her son Sunny, an eighteen-year-old high school senior, were sleeping.

Mamta came down the steps, which circled an inside fountain and waterfall. There was a rock garden that looked like a mountain, and at the top was a black, granite statue of a cross-legged Buddha.

Hindu philosophy is like an MBA class. The philosophy follows a very strict principle on an axiom level. It suggests, as is said in Latin, *Reductio ad absurdum*. Reduce all absurdities, i.e., all that can be negated is absurd and should be trashed. This also gives us a definition for truth. Truth is that which cannot be negated.

The pond below had lotus and water lilies. Amidst the lotus was a statue of Krishna. As Mamta came down the steps, she looked out through the greenhouse's glass entrance. She was trying to get a glimpse of the early morning sun. He was reluctantly trying to rise over the eastern sky. As she got a glimpse, she paused her activity, and with clasped hands and closed eyes, she made her salutations to him. Then she pulled out her wedding necklace, put it on her eyes, and kissed it. Turning to the statue of Krishna, she clasped her hands and then she did the same to the Buddha. This was a ritual she went through every morning. In the olden days when there were no artificial lights, people always credited the sun as the donor of sight to millions of people as he rose in the east. But for his illumination they were as good as blind.

Mamta went into the kitchen and started to make coffee in the percolator. After she got it going, she went into the adjoining powder room and brushed her teeth. The percolator was whistling at Mamta, and who wouldn't? As she was heading to the coffee pot, she updated the calendar on the top of the mantel. She tore off Thursday, June 20th, 1985.

The date was Friday, the 21st. Mamta poured coffee into her mug, which had an inscription, "World's Best Mom" and pictures of Sunny and Seshi. The nearby fax machine started to receive. She stood beside the fax with her coffee and read it as it was being printed. It was from Capricorn Travels and Bhupesh, a good friend of the family. It read as follows:

Dear Mamta Jee,

Your tickets will be given to you at the Toronto Air India counter. Your itinerary is attached. I wish you all a safe journey.

Dr. Mamta Rao

Miss Seshikala Rao

Master Sundereswara Rao

Air India Flight AI 181-First Class Seats 2A, 2B, and 2C

Depart Toronto 4.00 p.m. on Saturday June 22nd Arrive Montreal 6.00 p.m.

Air India Flight AI 182-First Class Seats 2A, 2B, and 2C

Depart Montreal 7.30 p.m. on Saturday June 22nd

Arrive London 8.30 a.m. on Sunday June 23rd.

Depart London 10.30 a.m. on Sunday June 23rd.

Arrive New Delhi 11.30 p.m. on Sunday June 23rd.

Asian vegetarian meals have been ordered on all applicable flights.

Indian Airlines will hand over your Indian Air tickets to you in New Delhi. All return flights can be booked at your convenience

PS: Mamtajee, my mother wants to come and see you for a physical as soon as you come back from India. – Bhupesh.

Mamta immediately sat down and replied that she would be back on July 15th and that Bhupesh's mother could come any day after July 15th. She also added that his mother should stay in their house in the guest bedroom since Mamta, as her doctor, knew what her diet should be and it would be more exact than she could get at a hotel restaurant. That's being a Good Samaritan.

Mamta poured another cup of coffee and proceeded to go to the bedroom. Rohit, as usual, was still in bed. This was another ritual of Mamta's. She wanted to be like her mother, very humble, loving, and ego free. Though Mamta's medical practice was twice the size of Rohit's, she never acknowledged that fact, not even when she was infuriated with Rohit, like she had been the other day.

Mamta had not seen the reason why they should travel from Toronto as opposed to Detroit. But Rohit was bent upon them leaving from Toronto because the tickets were twenty dollars cheaper than they were from Detroit. Mamta felt strongly that sixty dollars on three tickets was inconsequential. However, she allowed Rohit to have his way as she always did. She felt that like her mother, who took care of her father in every way, she too had to take care of Rohit.

What luck—one of the leading doctors in Cleveland and a very attractive lady, bringing your coffee to your bed. Rohit woke-up, clasped her hand, took the coffee with his other hand, and placed it on the side table. He pulled her close to him and was about to plant a very passionate French kiss on her lips. Mamta pulled away because she never liked to be kissed without Rohit having brushed his teeth.

Bolting in to the bedroom Seshi announced, "Dad and Mom are you guys up? Today is Friday and our flight leaves at three."

Both Mamta and Rohit just laughed.

"Sashi, our flight is not till tomorrow," said Mamta.

"Are you sure?"

"Yes, but now, since you are up, let's go buy few things for Grandma and Grandpa."

Sunny bolted in, a very handsome lad. "What about me? Sashi woke me up saying we were going to miss the flight."

"You two better get ready, we have a lot of purchases to make." Mamta, as she usually did, turned towards Rohit and smiled. "Is it OK if we go and do some minor shopping?"

Did she really need to have his permission?

Rohit, a splendid doctor himself, was handsome and a very loving father and husband. But when one saw him with Mamta one wondered if he was not a male chauvinist pig, the way he acted. However, you should not find fault with him since it was Mamta, who with her non-egotistical frame of mind and behavior, forced everyone to sympathize with her. Mamta knew it too and did enjoy the feeling of being completely dominated. Most Indian women know how to hang on to their husbands. With more than adequate love and overbearing affection they have their control over their husbands. Husbands usually cannot find a reason to object.

Mamta and Rohit had met at their college in Hyderabad. Both attended Gandhi Medical College. Rohit was doing his final year of medicine and Mamta was in her second year. The second year of medicine was the toughest of the program. It is in the second year they have to remember the names of all the bones and muscles in the body—literally everything associated with the body for their anatomy exam. So Mamta had *Grey's Anatomy* as her constant companion. Rohit teased her, always calling her Miss Grey's Anatomy. She always felt he was crude with his humor. One day at the bus stop he was waiting for the same bus and asked her if she knew who Miss Grey's Anatomy was.

She was very angry and taunted him by saying, "It's probably your mother."

He did not expect that. He kind of crawled out it by saying his mother's name was Bhanumathi.

"Then it definitely must be your wife's name, I am sure it is."

The examinations were held during the first week of April. The written examinations got completed and the oral examination was next. This was usually conducted by two professors, one from the local institution and other from another institution. The local professor wanted all his students to pass, while the external examiner was more realistic in giving grades. Mamta came out with very high distinctions in anatomy and indeed became Miss Grey's Anatomy.

The summer holidays had arrived. It was time for Mamta to go back to Grandpa's home where she could climb mango trees and live a carefree life for three months.

It was customary that when a girl had finished her second year of medicine, she usually was hitched as they call it in the U.S. Mamta's godfather showed up one day and explained to Grandpa that there was a very good match who was going to come to see Mamta that weekend. Both Grandpa and Grandma started to tell Mamta that it was for her own good that she should get married and that her godfather had already made sure that the boy was good with an impeccable family history. They did not have any medical problems of a hereditary nature and were quite well to do. They had a big house in Hyderabad and were regarded as elite.

The weekend arrived and so did the groom.

Mamta had been absolutely right when she'd said, "It definitely must be your wife's name."

Rohit and Mamta were now history as unmarried youngsters. The secret was that it was Rohit who had initiated the whole arranged marriage. He did not allow anyone to let Mamta in on the secret since he wanted it to be as she would have liked it…arranged by her grandfather.

Chapter Seven

PG continued with the original discarded storyboard.

At the international terminal, there was a passenger scheduled to fly to Montreal and then connect to Flight 182. He was checking his baggage and was insistent that it should be booked right through to New Delhi. The man was forceful with a thick accent, and seemed to know the rules well. He said he had no time and was in no mood to make a big deal out of it, however, he made it clear that the travel agent had told him he could book his baggage direct to India. The counter clerk called the manager and the baggage was cleared to book it straight through.

The gentleman was pleased and he politely thanked the manager. He said he wanted to smoke and asked if there was a smoking area. The manager indicated that he had to go to the curbside to smoke or outside the building. The man asked if he had time before the flight and was informed that the flight was boarding and that he should get his smoking out of the way quickly.

He got to the main exit and out in a hurry and headed to the garden patch across from the passenger drop off area, where he opened a pack of Indian beedies and lit one up. He sat on a bench there, as if waiting for someone.

Another gentleman walked towards him and asked for a beedi. He lit his smoke and sat beside him on the bench. "Did you put your luggage on Flight 003 and check it through to Delhi on 302 from Tokyo?"

The first man was affirmative with a nod of the head. They each smoked their beedi and walked together towards the car parking area. The baggage had made it but they did not.

※

It was Saturday morning in London. By a window overlooking Hyde Park, John Walsh, a writer from Cleveland, was smoking his State Express 555 and looking at the Londoners walking their dogs in the park.

His wife Joanne came from behind, put her arms around him, and caressed him. "It'll be fun visiting with all our old friends at Stratford, won't it?"

"Yes, it'll bring a lot of fun memories."

"The dinner at the theater is set late, so we won't have any theater-goers disturbing us, and all our friends will have finished their shifts."

"They all sprung for the dinner and they are only asking me to pay for the groceries: all labor is free, the restaurant is free, and it was nice of the Shakespeare Theater to let us have the fun evening."

"It might last all night and through into next morning."

"Well it will be worth every moment I spend with you."

They kissed. Not a Londoner saw them from Hyde Park; it was their private moment.

※

It was late at night in Cleveland. Mamta, Seshi, and Sunny had just returned from their shopping trip. Mamta, as usual, had bought the whole store for her favorite grandparents. Sunny and Seshi were also very generous with their gifts to all their cousins in India. It was customary for them to visit India and for all their cousins to come and raid their luggage. Each one took what they liked. Pants, shirts, and for Pete's sake, even boxer shorts. Last visit, some unlucky cousins whose sizes didn't match those of Sunny and Seshi, felt that they were unlucky. This trip Sunny and Seshi made sure they had all sizes in clothes so as not to let anyone feel that they had been left out.

They were all scrounging around for bags to carry the loot but couldn't find enough large bags. Their friendly Mexican gardener came to the rescue as he walked in with two overlarge, expandable canvas bags to hold anything and everything saying, "You remember Seshi Jee, when I was going to Mexico to visit my relatives last year, you took me to that Indian store on Chicago's Devon Street and bought me these two bags. You said they were like the fit-all, hold-all kind of bags."

"They were for you," commented Seshi.

"Now they are for you. Where would you get this kind of bag at this time?"

"But..."

"No buts and ifs, Miss Seshi. These are for you to take and once you are back you can return them to me."

"What's wrong with that?" retorted Sunny, grabbing the bags.

"I am selfish, Miss Seshi."

"Why?"

"I am sure Madam will not let you return these bags empty when you come from India—it's a win/win situation, isn't it?"

Mamta always explained any request with why she wanted it so. "Thank you, dear sir. Now we have only little time; we have to be all packed and ready to leave the house by nine. It's a trek of three hours with a stop at Niagara. They want us to check in at least two hours before the flight time, and that would be two p.m. So let's get cracking and packing."

Rohit always left everything to be taken care off by Mamta. "Leave me out of this, I have to drive and I need the rest. I am off to bed."

"You are a male chauvinist macho man, Dad," retorted the kids.

"You go to bed Doctor sir, I will help Madam and kids. What are we here for?"

Rohit walked away saying, "You do that Jose, I know I can count on that."

Everyone in the room laughed as if they knew that was going to happen. Now, the packing started in earnest. Sunny had to put on his favorite album by Engelbert Humperdinck. The number "Quando, Quando, Quando" was playing, and for some reason, with the décor of the house in the traditional Indian style, there was a hint of disharmony.

From a humongous glass jug, Sunny was drinking the grape juice he had just bought. Mamta was about to warn him that he might spill it all over the loot. Mamta was always ahead of everything that might happen, but this time she was late. As Sunny was trying to imitate Engelbert Humperdinck and got on the sofa and started to sing, he slipped and fell right on all the new clothes that were in a pile on the white carpet. The grape juice soaked all the clothes and there were three white faces instead of three brown. No one was able to utter a word.

Jose said, "Don't worry, it is only one in the morning and I will get them all cleaned, washed, and dried before you know it. You all just go to bed and leave everything to me."

"We have no other option, let's follow his advice," said Mamta. The telephone started ringing and Mamta ran to it and put it on speakerphone as if she knew whom it was from.

"Mamta," came from the speaker.

"Hi Tattayya."

"Hi Great-grandpa," echoed both the kids.

"We are eagerly waiting for you guys to show up."

"So are we," answered the three of them in unison.

"I sent invitations to all our kith and kin to come at the same time."

"You know it is my birthday," cooed Seshi.

"I know—that's why they are all coming. It will be like a big family reunion."

"That will be great," said the three in unison again.

"I am getting old and I don't know when my time will come; I want to spend as much time as I can with all of you."

"Don't talk like that, Grandpa, When I come I will take you to Gandhi Hospital for a complete checkup. All my professors owe me that for making their college a name in the U.S. by being one of the top physicians." Mamta acknowledged her accomplishments with only one person in her life and that was her grandpa. She felt that she owed him that. He had raised her ever since her mother passed away. She had lived with him and Grandma and believed that they were her everything. She always said that she couldn't live without them being around. Maybe that's why both her grandparents were still alive and in reasonably good health. She was happy that her children, Seshi and Sunny, were lucky enough to have their great-grandparents. For not having their grandmother, God's compensation was these two affectionate old people, who were always praying for them and thinking of their welfare.

"Great-grandpa, I am becoming a doctor too and I am going to specialize in geriatrics. I will take care of you two. You can come and live with me here in the U.S."

"God bless you, what more do I want?"

Sunny put in his two-cents worth. "Great-grandpa, I don't know what I will be…maybe an IAS officer like you."

"God bless both of you. I wish Rohit also joined you."

Rohit was on the line in the bedroom. "With these three gone, I have to be around to take care of things. I definitely promise you that I will come to see you ASAP." He didn't know what ASAP really meant in celestial terms. "I will also be there to take care of both of you. I have no one else but you five."

Rohit's grandparents had died when he was still very young. His parents had passed away even before he had his first child. That's why he and Mamta had named their children with his parents' names. His whole life now revolved around his loving wife, his two kids, and the grand old couple in India.

"I know I can count on you, Rohit. It must be late there—please go to sleep, you have a busy day tomorrow. We will be anxiously waiting for all of you."

They hung up the phone and Jose assured them, "Don't worry. Go and sleep—everything will be all right."

Gathering up all the clothes, Mamta apologized. "We hate leaving everything on you."

The evening sun shone on the face of the Statue of Liberty. New York was winding down, and PG was getting exhausted. So were Priya, Simrin, and Bob. The presentation was very emotional. PG could have won an Oscar for his method of presentation. He was fully immersed in the proceedings of the screenplay, as one could see his whole heart reflected in every word that he uttered. It was an experience that was new to both Bob and Priya. They had seen many people come through those doors, each one pitching some story or other, but everyone was interested in how much dough they were going to make as opposed to what they were serving or any intellectual high they might achieve.

No one there had the courage to tell PG that they'd had enough for one day.

But PG was exhausted himself. He paused for a moment and said, "Should we continue tomorrow?"

Bob did not want to say a word. Simrin was so engrossed in the proceedings she was just sitting there and taking the whole thing in. It was left to Priya.

"How about an early start at ten tomorrow?"

It seemed a good postponement to all concerned.

"That should be fine," PG agreed.

Getting up, Bob reinforced, "That's it—ten tomorrow."

"Can I get you something to drink?" Simrin enquired of PG.

"Diet Coke, please."

"I have an appointment at seven-thirty," remembered Priya as she was about to leave.

PG looked at her in anticipation of a question; he had that knack of doing that.

As she was about to leave, Priya stopped, hesitated for a moment, and piling up all her courage asked, "Did you know the Raos?"

"What do you think?"

"I bet you did."

"What odds?"

"I would bet my life on it."

The meeting was adjourned.

Soon after, Priya walked into the bar and found Monisha waiting for her in the far corner. Priya pulled a chair and sat in front of her friend. The waitress came to the table and Priya ordered a Molson Light. It was common for these two to come and have a drink or two before catching the late ferry across.

"How did your meeting go today?" asked Monisha.

"Good, he is actually writing about someone whom he knows very well."

"Really?"

"Yes I think he knows the Raos or that's what he calls them."

"Why do you think that he knows them?"

"How else would he know all the finer details of an Indian family life?"

"What do you mean?"

"He explained about a morning ritual where the wife removes the Mangala Sutra, presses them against her eyes, and prays to the early morning sun. She loves her husband so much that she is very submissive. It's like he met our parents and literally knows about all the happenings in our houses."

"He must have done a lot of homework."

"He has his soul in the story and he tells it as if he was present at every event like a fly on the wall."

"Wow I cannot wait to read it."

"It's getting to that time, let's scoot."

They both got up and started to walk towards the pier. New York was slowly becoming deserted and the night crawlers were coming out to find a warm place in the city in the dead of night.

As the ferry started to cross the Hudson they could see all the planes from Newark airport taking off into the night sky. It was one of those splendid nights when one can see the constellation Big Bear. In India they call it Sapta Rishis, the Seven Sages. In the Hindu wedding ceremony they show the three stars in the tail and ask them to see a tiny little star besides the middle one. They ask the bride and groom to be like those two stars side by side from ages ago to present and into future. Fulfill their affectionate voyage of life never to separate. I guess that's the Hindu way of life.

"See there is the big bear."

Priya said leaning on to the railing

"Don't ask me to look at Arundhathi star."

Priya smiled as she looked at Monisha

"I know what you are going to say next."

"Nothing just small talk."

Priya commented as she laughed

Monisha kind of felt trapped and tried to pull herself up

"Small talk from you? No way I know you better."

"Honestly no hidden agenda."

"OK. I will buy that."

"In India they…."

"There you go again."

"O. K. see that New York skyline. There is my office."

"The Skyline is majestic isn't it?"

"Yes it is…Yes it is."

"Aren't we lucky?."

"Yes Lucky. Thank our parents First Generation Immigrants."

Chapter Eight

Late August 2001

Bob was in the office early in the morning; he had to work on his poster. As Priya walked into the conference room, she saw a change in the poster, a large, oriental sword piercing the OM. The sword was shining and sparkling. Bob had already made the connection. Simrin walked in and felt uncomfortable looking at the poster. As PG arrived Bob was closing the blinds on the large bay window.

PG wasted no time as he picked his storyboards and waited to get started. As soon as his three audience members were ready, he started off.

It was the following morning, unusually late for Mamta. She hadn't gotten up on the early-morning sunrise schedule. Neither of the two kids were up either. It was Jose who knocked on the Raos' bedroom door and enquired, "Is it OK for me to enter, Madam?"

Mamta suddenly realized that she had been sleeping quite late. She'd had wild and bad dreams all through the night. She'd dreamt that there was a huge asteroid hurling towards Earth and there was nobody who knew how to divert it.

Rohit was still fast asleep beside her. She got out of the bed, put on a robe and announced, "It's OK. Come in Jose."

Jose came in with a pushcart with two full breakfasts on it. "All your stuff has been packed. I took the liberty to put some of your clothes in a carry-on bag, till you reach your village. You have your Indian wardrobe there. All the new things have been cleaned, dried, folded, and packed for the trip."

"Oh thank you, Jose. Are the kids up?"

"No Madam, I just woke them up and they've have their breakfast served also."

"Jose, I don't feel like going today and leaving Rohit."

"Why not? Do you think I will enjoy myself with you gone?" said Rohit as he was getting up from the bed.

"That's not it. I am just not comfortable going today."

"Madam, last night it was just an accident that the grape juice spilled."

"I have been having bad dreams, that an asteroid is hurling towards Earth."

Sunny walked in. "That was just a movie, Mom," he interjected, "that we saw last week. I want to go and enjoy the mango season and all that fresh coconut juice."

Seshi, who entered the room drinking her orange juice, joined in Sunny's urging.

"Well, four against one," said Mamta. "What can I do? The die is cast. Let's get ready and push ahead with full force."

"The die is cast." is a very original English saying. In the play *Julius Caesar*, Shakespeare uses those exact words when Caesar has to cross the river and attack Pompey, who in his absence has ascended the throne.

In reality, Mamta did not say it in that context. Veda Vyasa wrote *Mahabharata* in the year 6000 before Christ. In it, Dharma Raja, the ruler of the then-kingdom of Bharath, which is now called India, gambles and loses all his wealth and his kingdom. He continues to cast the dice in the hopes of regaining everything. In this process he loses all his brothers and himself, and finally he even pawns his wife, Draupadi, the Queen.

At that juncture, adding salt to the wound and saying, "The die is cast," the evil Dhuryodhana asks his brother Dhusyasana to bring Queen Draupadi into the court and disrobe her in front of the courtiers and elders.

The die was cast indeed and evil had its days numbered and so did the evil brothers who gambled with dice that were manipulated to give winning combinations.

Mamta indeed felt like Draupadi with no options except faith.

"The die is cast," John Walsh explained as he was sipping his morning cup of coffee. "We're leaving at about eleven-thirty. Let's take some time before and take in a show at the theater."

"What's playing?" asked Joanne.

"*Merchant of Venice,* my dear Portia."

"OK that would be fun before the party starts."

John Walsh and his wife Joanne were married and had two children. They had met at the theater ten years before and they were heading there for their anniversary party.

"It's a pity that we will be out there tomorrow, otherwise we would have met Mamta and the kids in London."

The doorbell rang and Joanne opened the door.

" Mr. and Mrs. Walsh?"

"Yes."

"I have a delivery for you."

"What is it, Joanne?" yelled John from the bedroom.

"It's a delivery of some sort."

"It's a flower arrangement, sir."

"From whom?"

"From whom else would it be?" Joanne said confidently.

"Not the Raos."

"Yes…Happy Anniversary to our dear friends, Joanne and John."

"Aren't they sweet."

"It reads, 'Wish we were there with you…Have a wonderful midsummer's night dream, as you like it, at Stratford. We will meet as soon as we come back from India. Mamta.'"

Joanne gave the bellboy a tip and closed the door behind him.

"Aren't they flying from Toronto?"

"Yes, they must have already started off to the airport."

"They'll pass through London tomorrow."

"Are all the bags packed and in the trunk?" Mamta enquired.

Jose replied, "Yes ma'am, all the luggage fit in the trunk."

"Did you count how many bags there are, Seshi?"

"I did Mom—six, two for each of us," replied Sunny.

"We are late, let's get going." So saying, Rohit came running out of the house, parked himself in the driver's seat of the Mercedes Benz top-of-the-line wagon, and asked, "Why are all of you delaying?"

"Yes Dad, we have been waiting here for the past half an hour," said Sunny. He, Jose, and Seshi started to laugh out loud while Mamta just smirked.

"Yeah, make fun of me. I can only depend on Mamta to take care of me."

"Yeah, mostly she babies you along, Dad. Grow-up," retorted the kids.

As he pulled away, Rohit called out, "Jose, I will be late tonight. Boy's night out."

Jose had a queer feeling in his stomach. As he was heading to his cottage at the back of the house, his father and mother were coming towards him.

"Jose, has Madam left? We just felt like seeing her for the last time before she took off to India."

"She will be back in three weeks, Papa."

"We know, but we felt like seeing her, don't ask why."

Jose smiled and said, "Yes, we will all miss her pleasant and pleasing manners and her blessings…She is an angel Mama, she is an angel."

Chapter Nine

Rohit was driving with Mamta in the front passenger seat. The kids, as usual, were in the back with their headphones, listening to Western pop music. Rohit had his own Indian film music from the fifties and sixties. What would "I Never Promised You a Rose Garden" sound like with a tabla and sitar background accompaniment? It's funny that the first-generation immigrants always freeze their memories at the point when they left their motherland. It's only when their kids, born Americans, come along that they start developing an identity of their own as first-generation Americans.

Mamta was wearing a red saree and a red dot on her face called a bindhi. She was absolutely astonishing in her color co-ordination and her beauty could carry it off. Seshi was wearing a designer blue-jean outfit. Sunny always wanted to play cricket, so he got himself clothed in his latest acquisition, a white pair of pants and long-sleeve white shirt. In those days it was a strict code by the English cricket circles. The three of them looked like the red, white and blue Americans.

It is difficult to be an American unless you are born in America because it is always difficult to handle freedom and the choices America so magnanimously offers. Freedom, as it sounds, is a very powerful entity. It imposes on one very many shackles, such as allegiance to the Constitution and social conformity as well. Many free countries do not understand that their citizens should mold their own futures and not necessarily those of corrupt, democratically elected officials. People usually get to a stage where they accept all inconsistencies as standard operating procedure. Mamta was heading to a country where corruption is taken for granted, and goodness in a person is taken as a weakness and not an asset. Many of her relatives used to take advantage of her soft, gentle behavior, considering it her weakness. Mamta knew it and brushed it off as an attribute of inadequate self-esteem and a psychological perversion created by a feeling of being one of the have-nots. Usually it manifested in an over-bearing personality, a high-handed approach, and brash speech with a pungent choice of words. Mamta always excused these people as ignorant, with inadept social behavior. Rohit was always the knight in the shining armor.

Rohit turned left onto the ramp, proceeding towards Interstate 90 East. As they got on the highway, Sunny felt uncomfortable since he remembered hearing something about an accident on Interstate 90. He could not recall if it was 90 East or 90 West. He didn't want to say anything, since he was the youngest and usually his dad ignored his views, which were of course radical like a Mohawk hairstyle. The traffic on the interstate was reasonably heavy. As they started to speed up and get into the flow, about five miles along the highway, lo and behold, there was a traffic jam and all traffic had come to a standstill. Rohit was in the interior lane with a concrete dividing wall separating it from oncoming traffic. With no other options, he came to a halt.

Mamta was kind of pleased that there was godly intervention into her travel plans. Sunny felt he was stupid not to have warned his dad of the news he'd heard. Sashi was so engrossed in her music she didn't care what was happening. Rohit was annoyed because he'd cut it too short to the flight time. As usual he remarked, "I said we had to be early and all of you delayed."

"It's OK dear, it's not a big deal if we miss it. We will take the flight tomorrow."

"That's the problem with you—you take everything easy."

"OK what else can we do now?"

"Mom is right, Dad," Sunny interjected.

"Dad is right," countered Seshi, taking off her headphones. "We should have left earlier in case of this kind of mishap."

"At least you are with me, Seshi."

"Yes Daddy, we should have woken you up at least an hour before."

"What are you saying?" Rohit was annoyed.

"You were late. We were all waiting for you."

Saying, "Let's all be calm and figure out what to do," Mamta came to the rescue of the family, as the controversy was slowly taking the shape of a major conflict. Hurt, Rohit got out of the car to get away from it for a while and started looking down the road to access the length of the stranded cars. They were at least five miles long. That was the visibility. He opened the door and said, "It's a bad jam. We may be here for hours."

Suddenly cars were being moved into the side lanes. They were being asked to move forward and backward in order to make space. As all this was going on, the weather decided that it had to participate in the proceedings also. For its contribution it clouded up that area with thick, dark, black clouds. Now there was a thunderbolt six miles ahead, roughly where there was a pile-up of cars. There had been a chain reaction that had caused the multi-car accident, and there were cranes trying to pry cars from the pile-up. One crane was sixty feet up in the air, lifting one of the cars from the pile. The lightning decided that it was the path of least resistance and landed squarely on it. The side riggers were out and made a perfect grounding system, and the crane lit up like a glowing structural torch.

The union of thunderbolts seems to have a very efficient communication system. As the first thunderbolt hit and dissipated, the crane operator got scared and was ready to leave his cab on the top of the crane, to get to a safe and sound area. The union was ahead of him; the thunderbolts started an assault on the crane, one after the other in rapid succession. It was like Heaven's fireworks display. The crane operator was halfway out when the second one hit. He was ejected from the mast of the crane like a ball of flame, but as luck had it, he landed in a pool of stagnant water beside the highway. He was safe.

The cars were starting to move in the heavy falling rain, and a cop tapped on the passenger side of the Raos' car. Mamta was a little unsure if she should slide her window down, but her doctor instincts forced her to open it. She said, "I am a doctor, can I be of any service, Officer?"

"Doctor, all accident victims have been already transported to the hospital."

"What happened, Officer?" enquired Rohit.

"Drunk driver caused a pile-up, but all are safe and sound in the emergency room.

The drunk driver is dead."

"How can we help you, Officer?"

"Jose called the chief and said you were on your way to Toronto to catch a plane."

"Yes…but Jose."

"He heard the news and called the chief; the chief is a patient of yours."

"I don't remember," Rohit said.

But Mamta remembered. "Chief Sadler, yes he was a patient of Rohit's and his wife Wendy was mine."

"Chief asked me to escort you out of the jam. Please follow my cruiser." So saying he went to his cruiser and put his lights on. Rohit wove his way through the small gap created by the cars, and started to follow the officer. Sunny thought it was cool. The cruiser went along the right shoulder and Rohit followed it. They soon came to the area where the pile-up was. The officer made sure they were allowed to bypass the obstructions and once they were free he came and wished Mamta and kids a bon-voyage.

As their car sped away from the scene, lightning was still striking the crane. As weird as it may seem, it looked as if it were trying to take revenge on the crane. Whoever said that lightning doesn't strike the same place twice? Yes, not twice but it can for six to eight times.

"It looks like we will be out of this storm center in ten to fifteen miles," Rohit explained, as if he knew what was ahead.

"Evil often takes advantage of good," was a profound quote from Mamta.

Mamta felt in her innermost heart that God was attempting to put barriers to taking this particular flight in her way. She was very uncomfortable but was unable to communicate it with logic or objectivity. She could only depend on her premonition. Some can accept premonition, but for someone else it can seem an illogical phobia. In this case, Mamta's good deeds were all ganging up against her to get her to take that flight. She was very contemplative and couldn't put her finger on this queer feeling that was eating her from the inside. She felt that she was putting her children into a compromising situation. Mother's instincts are always right aren't they? She literally did not know what to do but depend on God.

In *Mahabharata Draupadi,* Pandeva's wife, the queen, is in a similar situation. The evil king asks his brother that she be brought into the court, so she can be disrobed in front of everyone in the king's court.

In her mind, Mamta re-ran the events that followed.

Draupadi first resorted to the affection of a first cousin to get out of the situation. She explained that she was his older brother's wife and as such he should try to protect her.

Asking a mere human to do something out of his power?

When he refused because it was the king's order, she pleaded for his mercy and told him that she was in her menstrual period, and as such he should show mercy and pity and abstain from following orders.

When he refused she asked if she had been wagered before or after her husband lost himself. Her logic was that one who has lost himself doesn't have the right to make a bet any more.

This logic did not prevail either; she was dragged to the court by her abundant black hair, which was coiled around her like a black king cobra.

Once at the court she appealed to the family elders, who stood silent.

As a last resort she appealed to the queen mother and got nowhere.

Having no other options, as they pulled on her saree to disrobe her, she called upon God Almighty. As the story goes, God provided her with an endless saree, which could not be unwrapped, and foiled the attempt by the evil Dhuryodhana.

Mamta slowly began to feel that she was in the same predicament. No one was there to hear her plea and understand her premonition. She felt that she had to depend on God.

The thought came to her that if God wanted her, then what?

God, a name given to an entity no one has ever seen or heard from. Only some imposters claim that they have seen him and talked to him. It's like the story of the kid who said the king had talked to him. When all the villagers gathered to find out what he had said to the lad, it was revealed that the king had been riding his horse while this kid was playing in the middle of the street. The king was annoyed and said, "You stupid fool, get out of my way."

Yes, some people say God talks to them. Yeah, with his whole busy schedule, taking care of which meteor hits which planet and when? Meanwhile, The gravitational balance is being maintained so that no two planets will collide. Then there's making sure that the all life-giving sun doesn't run out of hydrogen fuel, lest we all freeze to death. He has come and talked to these folks so they can relay a message to convert everyone to God's way of life? This outlandish entity God had perplexed the Raos for all their lives.

Mamta remembered the ghazal[3] that Rohit had written and sung at one of the parties.

It was a party at Taj Ali Mahmood's house in Cleveland. He was a doctor who worked with Rohit. He was a practicing Muslim from India. Rohit's ghazals in Urdu were quite a hit in the cosmopolitan Indian community in Cleveland.

Mamta asked, "Rohit, will you do me a favor?"

"What is it, dear?"

"Please sing that ghazal you sang at Taj's party."

Usually Rohit never sang when someone asked him. He only sang when he felt like it. He said music was his way of relaxation and not for anyone else.

In this case, he made an exception. *"Aye bata mere dil merey dil Kiski khuda khuda hai."*

"Mummy, please translate the meaning as Dad is singing," requested Seshi.

Sunny reinforced the request. "Yes Mom, please."

Rohit continued to sing and Mamta translated the meaning

"Aye bata mere dil merey dil Kiski khuda khuda hai."

"Oh! My heart, my heart tell me whose God is the real God."

"Wo Khuda khuda hai tho merey hal , hal kya hai."

"If their God is real God, then what will happen to me?"

"Aye bata mere dil merey dil Kiski khuda khuda hai."

"Oh! My heart, my heart tell me whose God is the real God."

Mamta was questioning her own belief and if God really looked after each and every one of his species. Her major dilemma was why God allowed disparities in the human condition. If he was compassionate, he should treat everyone equally. Why were there so many children starving in Biafra while we here were overfed, obese, fat, and lazy when it came to proper exercise.

She went on a volunteer stint to Biafra after she returned she felt that despite of everything India was a little better off comparatively. Mamta's thought process was in over-drive, flying at the speed of light. She turned to Rohit and said, "Promise me that you will take care of yourself."

"Now don't go there please, it's only three weeks."

"I know. For my peace of mind promise me."

"Yes Dad, promise us that you will stay away from those friends."

---

3 A poem composed of couplets

Rohit had a few school buddies who loved to play cards, drink, and smoke, and have a jolly good time whenever they met. What they did was no worse than what kids do in most G-rated teen movies in America. Their idea of good time was just to get sufficiently drunk, and engage in horseplay like undisciplined teenage brats. Rohit claimed that he enjoyed an occasional indulgence with vulgarity. Mamta knew that he had been with that bratty group only once and that was enough for him. She also knew that he was only teasing them with his stated intentions. Both Sunny and Seshi were practically petrified that their dad was mortal and a day would come when he had to pack-up and take leave permanently. It was an incomprehensible thought for them.

"Promise!" shouted the three of them in unison.

"Three weeks of freedom for me," teased Rohit.

"No way!" shouted the kids from the back seat.

"Promise that you will take care of yourself," Mamta asked.

Rohit winked. "No way. I am going to have a fun time for three weeks."

"Then I'm not going to India, Dad," said Sunny. "It's not worth it to lose you."

"Neither will I go, Dad."

Mamta tried to appease Sunny and Seshi. "You know Daddy, he will be in India within five days, kids, just in time for his daughter's birthday for sure."

"I promised Grandpa that I will," Rohit explained

There was silence in the car for a little while. Everyone was in his or her own thought process and insecurities. Often people forget that there is only one truth in this world and that is: everyone who is born has to die one day and that is certain—some early, some later, but all do.

The car started to slow down on the Lewistown Bridge across the St. Lawrence Seaway as it came close to the immigration post at the Canadian border. Borders. If God wanted humanity to live separately, He would have created borders and compound walls. We build walls around cemeteries and Burning Ghats[4] also—how ironic. People don't want to go in there voluntarily. Once you are admitted there, definitely there is no known way to come out.

The car came to the checkpoint and slowed to a halt.

---

4 Cremation Grounds

As she was looking into the car, the immigration officer asked, "Citizenship?"

"American," answered Rohit.

Glancing at Mamta looking like an Indian in her saree, the officer asked, "Is she an American?"

"We both are naturalized citizens and the kids are born here."

"May I see some identification?"

Rohit passed out three passports to the officer and explained as he handed over his Ohio driver's license, "I didn't bring my passport but I have my driver's license."

"Purpose of your visit?"

"My wife and kids are heading to India from Toronto."

"Isn't Detroit closer to Cleveland?"

"Yes, but Air India doesn't fly from there."

"How long are you going to stay in Toronto?"

"I will be getting back tonight, for sure. I may grab some dinner in Gerrard."

"I hear the food is great there—Tandoori chicken."

"I wouldn't know that…I am a vegetarian," Rohit lied.

The Canadian officer was a lady and she could sense that Rohit was lying. She figured that he was trying to hide the fact that he ate chicken from his wife and kids. Mamta and kids saw no reason for Rohit to lie about eating chicken. Most Indians eat chicken. Mamta's perception led her to believe that the officer had picked-up on this. She anxiously awaited the next turn of events in the conversation.

"So you are a vegetarian and you don't eat chicken, is that right?"

Rohit always knew how to wiggle himself out of these kinds of predicaments. "Shoo…don't let the cat out of the bag, for Pete's sake." He put his finger on his lips, hinting that she should leave him alone. They all laughed except for Rohit, who acted serious and as if he was feeling victimized.

"Have a pleasant trip to India, and you, sir, have a delicious dinner…I mean chicken. Bye."

The car moved from the booth and Rohit remarked that they had very little time and headed towards the Lester Pearson International Airport. Queen Elizabeth Way was not busy and traffic moved pretty briskly. Sunny spotted the Air India plane over Lake Ontario, making its descent into Toronto Airport.

"There is the plane landing now!"

"Where? Let me see." Seshi moved towards the window nearest the lake.

"Well, what else is new? Indian standard time—it must have been late," Rohit said. Mamta answered, "Does it matter? It will still leave on time from here."

Seshi said in a mocking Indian accent, "What happened? Man, why are we stopping?" "Somebody must have pulled the chain," Sunny answered in an Indian accent, mimicking what usually happens on commuter trains in Bombay when they stop for no obvious reason.

The car got to the top of the bridge in Hamilton and started its downward trek towards Toronto. The CN Tower was within view, indicating that they were quite close.

Chapter Ten

After dropping off his family, Rohit came out at the lower level of Terminal Three at Lester Pearson Airport. He crossed the two vehicular-traffic roads and entered the parking garage. At his car, he opened the door and was about to get in when he noticed that two packages had been left in the back seat. He picked them up and raced back into the terminal to get them to Mamta. He didn't take the elevators but ran up two flights of stairs and straight to the immigration desk at departures.

He couldn't find Mamta and the kids—they had already left for the gate after passing through security. He was curious what the packages were and opened one to find a portrait of the four of them. The second had a photo of his two kids. He recalled that the two grand, old in-laws had requested that they send them two portraits, so they could hang them in their house. It was only last weekend the family had gone to an expensive photographer and done the sitting.

Rohit was panting and decided to sit in the coffee shop and take a breather. He
looked at the photographs and a very sad feeling came over him. He felt he should have not let them go without him.

The waitress brought him his coffee and placed it on the table. "That's your family, eh?"

Canadians have this trait of saying, "eh" with everything.

"They are on their way to India."

"I saw your son, he's handsome."

"My daughter is beautiful."

"Your wife is very attractive too."

"Yes, she is not only attractive, she is smart."

He put five American dollars on the table.

"We take it at par."

"Keep the change."

That was a very generous tip of three US dollars for a two Canadian-dollar coffee. Rohit quickly gulped his coffee and went back to his car. He put the two photos in the back seat. They were kind of looking up at the front seat where he was driving.

He drove out of the airport on to Dixon Road, crossed it, and stopped at the gas station and convenience store where he started filling the car. It was only a quarter empty. The gas filling only took few minutes. He went into the store and picked up a six pack of Molson beer, a bunch of salt and vinegar chips, and a PayDay candy bar and walked down to the counter to pay. The counter clerk rang everything up and asked, "Any gas purchase?"

"Yes, pump number six."

"That is six dollars and seventy cents."

"Do you…?" Rohit interrupted the clerk and then hesitated a minute.

She paused and enquired, "Anything else for you, sir?...I'm sorry, you were saying…?"

"Do you carry American cigarettes?"

"What brand do you want?"

"Kool, king-size, regular."

"That will be seven dollars and fifty cents more."

"What?" The last time Rohit smoked they had been two bucks.

"The taxes here are obnoxious."

"I guess they *are* expensive. How can people afford to smoke?"

"I don't know, I think really they should ban alcohol."

"I agree."

"Do you want them, sir?" she asked, for reinforcement of the sale.

"Yes please, with a book of matches."

"We don't give out matches anymore."

Rohit was annoyed. "Don't act like my wife, who doesn't want me to smoke."

"I can't help it, sir. We sell lighters, do you want one?"

"Do I have any other choice?" He chose a lighter and flipped it onto the counter in disgust. It was his guilt feelings that were taking shape in this form. He had promised his dear wife he would take care of himself.

"That'll be thirty-three dollars and thirty-three cents."

"Here is fifty dollars, keep the change."

"These are American dollars and with the exchange rate they are fifty-five Canadian dollars and fifty-five cents. You really mean it?"

"So what?"

"You're giving me a twenty-two-dollar and twenty-two cent tip for a thirty-three-dollar purchase?"

Rohit always did that just to get a reaction. Once he had gone with Seshi to a car dealer who was known to be a racist. The dealer prided himself as the "Boss Man." Of course, everyone who knew Rohit knew of his pranks. He went in and the dealer walked up to him and assessed him to be a Mexican. Then he proceeded to treat him as such and said, "hola buenos días."

"*Namaste, Sala.*"[5]

"What did you say?"

"*Tum mey Hindi baat karna nahi aataa?*"

"Oh. Hindu I don't know."

"Pouvez-vous parler français?"

"French I don't know."

"Mandarin?"

"No."

"Telugu?"

"No."

"Tamil?"

"No!"

"Japanese?"

"*No no!*"

"*Deutsch?*"

"No! No! Only American."

"*Anglais?*"

"No, *no Anglais*! Only American!!"

"English?"

---

5 "Greetings, bloke" in Hindi.

"No! No English! Only American."

"OK then, American it is."

The dealer realized he had been stumped. "Can I be of assistance?"

"Sure, what is the difference between American and English?"

"Spelling like N I T E."

"K N I G H T? Like the round table?"

"No, it's NITE like dark after six p.m."

"Oh…N I G H T night."

"Yes, how can I help you?"

"I want to buy a car."

"Do you have a model in mind?"

"*Big* car. Big car that's it…*Big* car."

"How big?"

"Bigger than my neighbor's."

"That doesn't tell me anything."

"The biggest you got."

"The biggest I have is a truck."

"Family truck, that will be fine, but *big*!"

"You know you are at a Benz dealer?"

"*Big*…that's it *big*!"

"OK, it's our SUV."

"That's fine, SUV it is."

"What options?"

"Loaded!"

The dealer hesitated. "Loaded? You mean everything?"

"Yes, like first class airplane seats."

"That will cost you a lot of money."

"OK, but *big loaded,* like every seat with its own VHS and stereo system, so everyone is free to see and hear what they want."

Seshi was enjoying the fun.

"Let me get you a price." He went into his office and started to work out a price. His Sales assistant, an African American, asked him what was going on.

"I got this Hindu wants a big car loaded; it's a waste of my time trying to figure all this out. Why don't you handle this and do your Massa tricks and shuffle all you want."

"OK, then I get the commission and credit on the sale." the African American salesman insisted.

"If he buys, then you get it, but he's just window shopping."

"I get the commission and credit for the sale," he reiterated.

"Yes, yes, he's yours."

The African American salesperson was named Sam; he knew who this customer was and had no doubts about what he could do. "Dr Rao, my name is Sam. I will be helping you with your purchase."

"OK Sam, did he tell you what I wanted?"

"Yes sir, he did. It's our top of the line SUV. It has everything you want with individual stereo systems, but individualized DVD players aren't out as yet. We will give you VHS players."

"That's bad."

"May I make a suggestion?"

"Please do."

"Once you get the delivery, I know a place where they would install it. The total comes to seventy-three thousand fifty dollars, and how would you like to pay for this?"

"Cash."

Sam figured out what was happening and smiled mischievously. "That will be fun, watching my boss dance all over," he said with contempt. "Thank you very much for giving me an opportunity to watch the fun."

Rohit already priced it and knew the exact amount. He had it in hundred dollar bills in a doggy bag. Handing it over, he said, "Sam this is seventy-four thousand fifty dollars and the thousand is a tip for you. Make sure they count it right."

"Thank you very much, sir, I will. First let me get the contracts for you to sign, and get my boss to start counting."

Rohit knew the fun had just started.

"Sam what in the hell are you telling me?" said his boss.

"There is $ 74,050 in the bag—$ 73,050 for the car and 1,000 tip for me."

"This is crazy, it must be a mistake."

"No it's not a mistake, there is really cash in the bag."

"Do as I say, take him and his daughter, make them sit in the conference room, and close the door. Ask them to wait there."

"Why?"

"You want to work here, boy, then do what I tell you."

Sam went to Rohit and apologetically asked them to wait in the conference room.

As they were being led into the room Rohit said, "Sam, just play along, let's have some fun."

"OK."

Sam went out back into the office. Boss Man was calling the local sheriff's office and telling them there was a guy who looked like someone who had robbed a bank and that they had to come and arrest him immediately. As the boss was making the complaint, his daughter Mary walked in and got involved in the proceedings.

The sheriff's office sent three cruisers and the sheriff himself was in one of them. The sirens were going and they arrived at the dealership with a lot of pomp.

"They are coming to arrest us, Dad," Seshi remarked.

"Let's see," Rohit said, looking out of the window. There was only one door to the conference room. "We cannot even escape, there is no emergency exit."

They both laughed.

Boss Man explained the situation to the sheriff. "I knew he was a crook the minute I laid eyes on him."

"Where is he?"

"Like Bonnie and Clyde, they must have robbed the bank."

"Did you ask them their names?"

"No."

"Did you ask him where he got the money?"

"No."

"What makes you think he would have robbed the bank?"

"He is not white."

"Is he an African American?"

"No."

"Is he a Hispanic?"

"No."

"Then what is he?"

"I guess a Hindu."

Understanding his racist behavior, the sheriff said, "You can't just brand people like that."

"Dad, I always told you all people are equal," Mary butted in.

"Let's go and talk to them and find out," said the sheriff.

"I locked them in the conference room."

"What did you do? Lock them in? You're in a lot of trouble if they're legit, you know that," cautioned the sheriff as they all walked to the conference room and opened the door.

The sheriff entered first, followed by Boss Man, his daughter, and then Sam.

Seshi addressed the sheriff. "Hi Uncle."

The sheriff smiled at Seshi and then addressed Rohit. "Hi Doctor Rao."

Rohit nodded at him and turned to Mary. "Hi Mary."

Sam eased the situation. "May I get your papers, Dr. Rao?"

Boss Man was speechless.

Mary went to Seshi, hugged her, and said, "Dad, don't you recognize Seshi? She always came to our house to do homework when we were in school."

Boss Man was still speechless.

Rohit said, "We wanted to escape and run for the car, Sheriff, but this room doesn't have an emergency exit. Isn't that a violation of the fire code?"

Boss Man came to his senses. "This is just a storage room and it's not normally occupied."

"Aren't you the fire chief also, Sheriff?' Rohit asked in a taunting manner.

The sheriff glared at the car dealer. "How many times have I told you to get an exit from this room?"

"But…" Boss Man tried to explain.

"He got a hefty mark-up on my car and he got it in cash, so he should get the door completed within two weeks," said Rohit.

"Yes, the doctor is right," said Boss Man. "I will get it done—we have a thousand-dollar tip."

"Hey! that was my tip for working with the doctor," said Sam.

The Boss Man replied, "We will see about that."

"You tried to get him…arrested!"

Boss Man interjected quickly, "We'll get him his *big* car right away. Sam, get the inventory of colors."

"Next time you call me…" the sheriff warned.

"I will check everything out first," Boss Man replied.

Did he mean it?

This is our problem in America. As much as we pride ourselves on the melting pot concept, we brand people. Maybe it's because we branded our animals when we first came to America. We branded the slaves as we brought them from Africa. We are perceived by the rest of the world as people with fixed notions and no flexibility. It's our way or the highway. Why do we think we are sure of everything that there is in the world? Why do we think we have the right answers? Why do we think we are the saviors of the world, when we have amidst us, people like Boss Man? We cannot accept anything or anyone other than our own. Is this what a Christian way of life is? Somewhere we are missing the boat, aren't we? Our majority believes in our Constitution and our form of government, and as such, we put up with whatever is dished out whether we agree or not. We believe in our president and his capacities despite his human frailties.

Rohit had his own frailties. After he bought his cigarettes at the airport, he got into his car and took a left and then a right onto 427 South, hoping to take the QEW to Coxwell, then on to Gerard and its Indian marketplace. He put on one of those old Indian film songs, from a case with a picture of a debonair hero, who was chasing a damsel all over Shimla's picturesque Himalayan slopes with just a hint of snow. The hero and heroine were dressed in colorful costumes and wearing wool sweaters with beautiful designs on them. The song blasted from the speakers. The traffic was heavy and fast. Rohit fumbled through the shopping bag he'd put on the passenger-side seat. As he was trying to retrieve something from it, his car started to swerve into the other lane. The Canadian driver in that lane honked vehemently to get Rohit's attention while cursing the dumb, stupid, American driver. He passed Rohit and as he overtook him, showed him the middle finger. Rohit's blood got hot, and as he had the better car, he ramped up his speed, and by the time he caught up with the Canadian they were on the QEW, heading east. Rohit then proceeded to overtake the other driver and getting his attention, showed him his middle finger with his tongue sticking out of his clenched lips. He had his tit for tat, I guess.

Now he was approaching the downtown area and could see the CN Tower and the Sky Dome. Making sure he was in his lane this time, he opened his pack of Kools, pulled out a cigarette, and used his newly acquired lighter to light it up. He cranked his window slightly open. It made a whistling racket; however, it blended well with the loud music. As he was trying to change lanes, he looked over his right shoulder and saw the framed photos of his wife and kids. He quickly slid open his side window, discarded the cigarette, and began to park his big car on the narrow shoulder of the QEW. He was annoying each and every driver on the highway, but he didn't give a damn. Once he got parked, he got out, took the two framed photos from the back seat of his car, opened the trunk, and placed both of them the spare tire compartment. Then he closed the trunk. He pulled out another cigarette, lit it up, and started to smoke as he enjoyed the view of the CN Tower. He felt that he was on top of the world.

The traffic on the QEW slowed down to a snail's pace, due to the "disabled" car on the narrow shoulder. "Do you need assistance?" enquired a passing car driver. Little did he know what was happening.

"Just a little over-heated engine. Should be OK now," lied Rohit. He got back in his car with the cigarette between his right-hand fingers, and fumbling with his left hand, started the car, put it in drive, put on the right blinker, and merged into the slow-moving traffic, before speeding up towards the east. In his rear window he saw the CN Tower and the sun setting in the west with a reddish, orangish glow and some unspecific brush strokes of violets, blues, and streaks of green. Above all of them were the white trails of jet engine exhausts from planes heading west. Some had only one streak, suggesting that a 737 had made them. Some had two streaks, so Rohit guessed 727, and quite a number had the four streaks of a Boeing 747. It was that time of the day when all the 747s took to the sky with 400-plus passengers in each, heading in all different directions to long-haul destinations.

Rohit was too much on his own Cloud Nine to even notice the splendor of nature. He was enjoying his Kool.

His destination at Gerard was reached and he parked his car on one of the side roads and locked it up. Lighting another cigarette, he walked toward where all the shops were. He seemed to be enjoying his sudden anonymity. That's why this all-powerful entity we so loosely term as God, while using him for our own secret agendas, is probably the only witness to each and every thing one does. The other witness is the never-ending continuum of time that perceives all and keeps it a secret.

Rohit stopped at Bombay Chat House. He ordered a faluda. It's an Indian milkshake made with a hint of rose water, sweet syrup, and a scoop of vanilla ice cream. Once he had it, he got in the car and started to drive back to Cleveland.

Suddenly there was an interruption of his freedom in the form of a brand-new invention: the car phone, which started ringing.

"Don't you know I am off today?" he said aloud. But so he wouldn't be impolite, he answered the phone after a couple of rings. This is a social etiquette we all live with; we cannot even say what we mean. Anticipating that it was a call from the hospital he answered, "Dr. Rao here."

There was a kind of sobbing from the other side. It made him uncomfortable and unsure of himself and he felt very guilty. He was ashamed of his mental gymnastics. At the same time, his other side of his brain assured him that it was OK. I guess he fit into the category of the rich.

"Who is this?" he asked. He damn well knew who it was. He needed to have some time to bring his frame of reference to his role as loving husband and father. Don't get me wrong —Rohit was the best in his performance of these duties, with the exception of his wild imagination, which had a way of taking him to the far reaches of the universe as well as to the far reaches of untrodden ways of human imagination.

The sobbing continued...

"Mamta, what is this? You are a physician and you should be strong. The kids will be upset. What is wrong?"

"Well...well...I...miss you." The sobbing continued and with a heavy stutter, she said, "I ...I...love you...I only loved once in my life and it happened to be you."

"I love you and kids very much, Mamta, you are the only ones for me. My whole world is the three of you."

"I know that, but for some reason I don't feel good leaving you and going."

"You are going to see your Tata, whom you adore."

"I know, but still I miss you..."

Rohit suddenly felt very uneasy and his real emotions took the main stage. Human beings are always gifted with two layers of emotions: one superficial and the other entwined with the heart. Brain activity always keeps the emotions that are entwined with the heart in the innermost depths of the emotional bank account. Actually they are locked up in the safe deposit vault of Fort Knox. We need to get through the main guards, then the main doors, and then with the gate keeper and a set of keys, we open the safe to pull out the most precious of our intimate emotions. I don't know why there is a veil on these feelings when it comes to the male gender. They hide them as if they are so precious that they can't share them. Most of the time it is too late before they dig them up to serve them on a silver platter.

This was such a situation and Rohit was being put to the test. He took refuge in logic.

"Mamta, you will be in your favorite place where you grew up with your favorite two people, your Tata and Ammumma. You can eat all the jackfruit, jamun, and mango and drink all the coconut nectar you like."

"All without you. It doesn't make any sense."

"I am coming in a few days to join you."

"I know...I know...I love you."

"Mamta...listen...you are all I've got...I love you." There was silence for a while and Rohit broke it up with, "I love you, Mamta...I love you, Mamta."

The vault was open. He felt very uneasy. He couldn't help thinking that he should have let the whole family go as it was planned earlier. He wanted them to have a good time for a week more, ahead of him coming. This he felt he owed to Mamta, to let her spend some time with her grandparents, who had raised her and taken care of her after she was deprived of her mother's love and affection at a very tender age. Sometimes God can be cruel.

Rohit cleared his stuffed-up nose and the lump in his throat, and Mamta realized that she had entered her husband's inner sanctum. She knew how much her husband loved her even though he didn't always say it loud. She didn't want to burden him with her illogical fears, so she immediately changed the subject. "I will save the best jamun for you."

Rohit's vault was open. "I love you...you always save the best for me, Mamta."

"I saw these phones in the plane and wanted to see how they work. And at the same time I wanted to say hello to you. Where are you?"

"I am on the way to Niagara." Rohit realized that she'd caught on to him.

"We are just flying over Manistee in the upper St. Lawrence."

"We were on vacation there."

"That big rock in the Atlantic Ocean."

"Do you remember we were very naughty on the beach?" teased Rohit.

"Shoooo, the children are here."

As if the kids could hear the conversation through their headphones.

"Sunny should know he was launched there," laughed Rohit.

That did it. There was a click and the conversation ended.

Rohit continued to drive as he thought about the three of them. As much as he claimed that he really didn't care, he had already started to miss them and was looking forward to going to India to surprise Seshi for her birthday.

Chapter Eleven

It was eleven a.m. Saturday morning. The usual hustle and bustle was not there in London traffic. The British had taken a little while to get caught up with the American system of working five days and having a two-day weekend for fun and games. They were used to royalty telling them what to do and they did it without question for a long time. As they say, what else does the commoner know than his fish and chips? The United States is the only country that knows when to work and when to play, and most importantly how and what to play. In Britain, the commoners worked their asses off. Nobility was bestowed, based on whims and fancies or whomever the royals wanted to be associated with. So you could be and become a sir, a count, an earl, or a knight if Henry the Eighth decided that he liked your looks. In conclusion:

The commoners worked seven days. Royalty played cricket for five days and took rest for two days. Then they played cricket for five days again. What a life in England—something to envy.

Drinks—Lunch—Tea—Cricket.

For the commoners, it's: Work—Pub—Beer–Soccer—Beer—Pub—Beer—Pub—Beer recurring in mathematical sequence.

Royalty was resting, commoners were working, and Americans were exercising by running round and round in Hyde Park.

Joanne stood on the balcony of the hotel looking at her Prince Charming running round and round in the park like a hamster in the wheel. She was happy and very much so because she had landed a loving, affectionate person—a literal family man.

John came down under the balcony and said, "What doth you say, dear Princess Julia?"

There was a recognizable stutter in PG's narrative voice. Priya and Simrin picked up on it; however, Bob was pre-occupied looking at his poster. PG's eyes were suddenly full of tears, as if it was his way of foreshadowing the coming events.

"It's eleven darling," Joanne called down, "The die is cast to leave at eleven-thirty."

"I'll be in. It will take only a minute to shower and get ready."

As John started his trek back to the room, the doorbell rang. Joanne opened the door to find a huge flower arrangement with red roses, blue carnations, yellow chrysanthemums, violets, five different colors and shades of hibiscus, and a lot of green foliage with American and British flags on the sides. The bellboy carrying it was completely hidden behind it.

Joanne was speechless. This was a humongous flower arrangement.

The bellboy said, "Mrs. Walsh, I lost my words when it was given to me to be delivered. I thought it must be from a very special person to a very special person."

Joanne still was in a daze.

"May I bring it in Mrs. Walsh?" the bellboy asked.

"Sorry, please yes, yes, please do."

Why do people become incoherent when faced with a pleasant surprise? Joanne immediately checked to see whom the flowers were from. As she was about to read the card, John walked in, completely drenched in sweat and stinking like a dog. At least that's what she usually told him after his usual workout, and she always asked him to go to the shower immediately before he did anything else. She didn't want him around anywhere, especially around the children when they were young. John used to comment every time that he felt that he was talking to his departed mother. When he was young he used to come straight from his run into the kitchen, to raid the fridge and get some of the tasty pies his mom had made. She used to say, "You stinking dog, go get showered before you touch anything."

The bellboy was anxiously waiting for his tip.

Joanne saw the card and read it aloud in absolute ecstasy. "Without you, life is a wasted journey. With you, it's a bed of roses of different colors. To my dearest Joanne, from only yours forever, your hubby, John."

She turned around and saw the stinking dog in sweaty shorts and sneakers, looking like hell. There were tears in her eyes. The flow managed to get out and run in streaks down her rosy cheeks. She didn't wait to wipe them because they were happy tears. Tears are of many kinds: some that are happy, some that are angry, some that are sorry, some that are sad, some that are melancholy, some that are bitter, some that are born out of anguish. We just have a tendency to shed tears.

"You stinking *dog!*" So screaming she dashed to him and hugged and kissed him.

John was hesitant as to what to do in this bizarre, out of the norm, event. "I'm all sweaty," he said meekly.

"I don't care. I love you, John, I love you."

John was relieved, immediately kissed her passionately, and soon both were in a passionate encounter. He lifted her up and took her into the adjacent bedroom.

The bellboy was just ignored. He didn't know what to do, so he slowly got out of the room and closed the door behind him.

The four walls of the hotel room were so well soundproofed that no one could hear the sounds of what was going on in the closed quarters. Squeaking springs? The norm was broken.

"Does this mean I can…"

"No! No way! The rules still stand." Joanne was herself again.

"No fair," said John

"Let's shower together and get ready," compromised Joanne.

"OK," John agreed.

Marriage is a game of compromises isn't it?

There was a moment of utter silence when they just embraced each other and lay there on the satin sheets of the hotel bed. The silence was then broken with a vehemently loud hot shower. You could have heard them giggling and whispering sweet nothings to each other if you had been a fly on the wall.

Why do we call them sweet nothings?

The bellboy was absolutely annoyed with Cupid.

Suddenly, from the shower, there was a scream—the kind that meant *I forgot something*. Having worked as a waitress, Joanne knew what it meant when your gut said it was big tip time. As if she had blundered, she came running out of the shower, not even noticing that she was stark naked. She entered the living area, grabbed a twenty-pound note and said, "Here is your tip."

Not knowing what was going on, John followed her and standing behind her said, "Thank you ma'am."

They were both stark naked. She suddenly realized that she was wearing nothing and that John also was in his birthday suit. Her modesty took over and involuntarily her two arms went into a cross form, covering her upper body. She stood in the middle of the large room like a sculpture, with her head tilted slightly to her right. It was a modest pose, which could have inspired William Wordsworth to write a sonnet and Somerset Maugham to write a novel. William Shakespeare, I guess, would have had Henry the Fourth chase her all over with a chicken leg in his hand and a mouth full of gravy.

John just stood there and just gazed at her like she had been carved by Michelangelo. Realizing what she had just done, she slowly moved close to him and let him wrap himself round her and protect her like her knight in shining armor.

"Dear, it's time. Let's get dressed and get going," he murmured.

"Do we have to go?" she said lovingly.

Men being as pragmatic as they are, John said, "We can't keep them all waiting," in a soft, romantic voice.

They each dressed exquisitely and just before going out, kissed each other and expressed that they loved each other. After the door was closed behind them, Joanne reminded John that they had forgotten their bag of changes, just in case something spilled on their clothes. He went back in, grabbed the bag, and proceeded to follow his show stopping wife to the top of the winding staircase in the hotel.

They looked like royalty standing at the top of the stairs and as far as they were concerned they were on the top of the world. Royalty? What really constitutes royalty? Clothes? Riches? Palaces? Courtiers? Jesters? Authority? Ego? Guards? Ancestry? Kingdom? Or Acceptance? As if specifically for this royalty, the elevator, I am sorry, the *lift* music was playing the song "Top of the World" sung by Karen Carpenter. John and Joanne tapped their toes to the beat of the song.

The bellboy noticed a twenty-pound note in Joanne's clenched fist. He dashed up the stairs, grabbed the bag from John, and stepped down three stairs before them. Then he turned around, stopped, and said, looking at Joanne in her rich beautiful, elegant gown, "Happy anniversary."

She put the twenty in his hand. "Thank you for understanding and leaving us alone."

John added another twenty.

The bellboy's confidence in love, Cupid, sex, and romance was reinforced and he involuntarily said, "Ma'am, I guess my mind is made up. I am going to propose to my sweet Mary today. Now I know what I have been missing for the past ten years."

"Congratulations!" cried John and Joanne.

"Your limo is waiting."

The big grandfather clock in the lobby started to chime like the Westminster Cathedral bells. The old lady who had won a bet when they got married was in the forefront.

"This is new. What old lady? What bet?" Priya enquired.

Priya's remark brought Bob and Simrin out of the daze they were in, listening to the emotional yet sensitive and heart-wrenching presentation. They did not care—they just wanted it to continue.

"Let him continue." Bob mandated and PG continued.

The hotel lobby was filled with people as if they were courtiers. John and Joanne started to come down the stairs hand in hand. A cameraman was taking flash photographs in the lobby. One of the flash bulbs went off with a big bang like one of the bombs to which London was accustomed. Joanne suddenly hugged John and whispered, "I'm scared."

"It's just a flash bulb."

"I feel something is not right."

"You need a drink, that's all."

They got into the limo and it drove away and cruised down M4, but instead of turning towards Stratford, it took a turn away from their destination. John and Joanne were in each other's arms in back of the limo, listening to music from the sixties and seventies.

The car stopped and the door opened. Joanne was confused.

"I arranged a gondola ride for you," said John.

Joanne was pleasantly surprised.

"It will be a forty-five minute ride on the romantic River Avon."

They went through some of the thick bushes and there was the gondola with the driver clad like the Italian gondoliers. There was a musician with an accordion. A beautifully arranged mattress and pillows were arranged for them to relax on.

"This is like a fairy tale, " Joanne commented as she was getting into the gondola. The gondolier started to navigate the River Avon. Joanne, for the first time, began to see the beauty of the countryside where she'd grown up. It's funny that we grow up accepting for granted everything that is there. We take for granted that our parents will be there for us forever. In all Joanne's happiness she suddenly realized that the cottage where she'd grown up had been on the banks of the Avon. It wasn't there anymore and nor were her dad and mom. She was just about to get depressed at the thought of not having anyone.

It's said marriages are made in Heaven. God matches people that are compatible to each other if we listen to his voice through our consciousness.

Consciousness always leads us on the right path but human beings have this tendency to veto its prescription because we think we know better.

John and Joanne listened to their inner voices and so their union was made in Heaven. That's why John knew exactly what was going on in her mind. He figured that she was brooding about her family. He knew enough to get her out of that spiral spin and gently gave her a peck on her cheek. She knew enough to know that he had figured out her thought process. What else did she want other than a loving husband who thought he was PG Wodehouse and thought the world of her? He put his arms around her, pulled her close to him, and asked the musician, "Please sing 'Al Di La' from *Rome Adventure*."

The man started to sing the song just like the original, with his accordion as a complement, and the music made the lovers close their eyes and thank God for making their marriage in Heaven.

The green meadows felt fortunate to be witness to a happy Romeo and Juliet saga, and not what they were used to playing at the RSC. There were some meadows where sheep were grazing and some meadows where there were cows. Once in a while the gondola passed through the thick, wild bushes. Occasionally, the river flowed underneath a bridge. Usually the bridge was built of bricks and had a narrow passageway to let the boats pass by one at a time. Most of the passersby on the bridges were curious what a gondola was doing on the Avon. This was un-British. There were some young lads with plaid shirts sitting on small boulders and casting fishing lines into the river. They looked like paintings. The whole countryside was curious and talking about the gondola on the Avon.

Stratford-on-Avon was in sight. The Royal Shakespeare Theatre could be seen majestically standing on the banks of the Avon. Near it there were swans swimming. Stratford is the birthplace of William Shakespeare. It is tucked away in the beautiful countryside of rural Warwickshire. The Stratford business district is in Oldie English style and is quaint. The RSC, the Royal Shakespeare Company's grand theater, is a red brick building with an elliptical dome on the top. It has a few steps in the front to enter the building. Once you are inside, to the left the corridor leads to a restaurant for the patrons of the theater. The restaurant is a long, wide, eating area with a glass wall looking onto the River Avon. There are some benches where one can sit and look at the swans swimming. Alongside the river is an outside porch that runs the length of the building with seating for people to eat.

As the gondola arrived at this place, everyone knew that it was the time and gathered at the glass wall of the restaurant to witness the alighting couple. This was a marriage that really had taken place there. All waitresses dream of similar happenings. Joanne was the lucky one there. Many a waitress had lost her virginity in pursuit of the perfect one. As the couple came ashore, one of the new waitresses was waiting with a loaf of bread, and she gave it to Joanne. Joanne knew exactly what it was for. She slowly put her arms round John's waist and took him to one of the benches by the river. They sat on the bench and kissed. There were huge sighs, and oohs and aahs from all the people watching from the restaurant.

"Isn't it very romantic?" one said.

"They are meant for each other, " another said.

"They are truly in love with each other," a third one said.

"Watch, all her real friends will show up," said Joanne's friend.

All the swans around came to the bench and started courting the couple with their own swan language. Looking at the spectacle, the actress who played Portia in *The Merchant of Venice* showed-up, looked at the river and commented, "So, Joanne has arrived."

"Yes, she has, with her Prince Charming," answered Joanne's friend.

"Do you think there is anyone else like them in this whole world, so madly in love with each other?"

"Last time she wrote to me that: there actually is one couple."

"Really?"

"Yes, she said it was Mamta and Rohit, their family doctors."

"Are they coming to this event?"

"They were but they had to go to India to attend to her grandma."

"That's too bad we won't be seeing them." the spinster that played Portia commented.

John and Joanne left the riverbank and walked through the main street. Everyone in town knew that there was a party for them. There were not three steps taken before people stopped them and enquired about their welfare, and were so intimate with Joanne that it spoke volumes about her skills in interpersonal relationships. There are only few people that are equipped and adept enough to maintain such good relations with people whom they have not met in years.

The restaurant had decorations wishing them Happy Anniversary. The place was bubbling with a lot of joy and admiration for one of them who had made it and was happy. The only thing missing was their two children.

The dinner was a buffet because most of the servers were guests. The RSC artists had prepared a medley of songs from Broadway shows in honor of the couple. The tunes encompassed shows like *Westside Story, Oklahoma, Pajama Game, Cats,* and for Joanne, tunes from her favorites: *Phantom of the Opera, Brigadoon* and *The Sound of Music*. The guests sang along with the group. As the dinner was coming to an end, the guests started clinking their glasses. John said that he'd been waiting for that and he grabbed Joanne and gave her a passionate kiss. Looking at the willingness from them, the guests did not clink their glasses anymore. Instead, they asked for a speech from them.

The head waitress, who was a friend of the couple, and had been in the restaurant when they met, said, "Wait a minute, there are some people here who want to say a few words before it's John's and Joanne's turn."

All the guests clapped as she started to emcee the evening. "First of all, let me introduce to you the winner of the bet twenty-odd years ago, Mrs. Karen Longworth."

Mrs. Longworth was in her eighties and walked with a stick. She got up from her seat and slowly came up to the microphone. The disc jockey was getting prepared to start the dance session. Some of the male employees of the restaurant were removing some of the tables so as to make space for the dance. Mrs. Longworth stood magnanimously on the small stage, looked around the audience, and made eye contact with every one there. She must have attended the Toastmaster Club. She started off her speech: "Happy Anniversary. Today is a very special day for me. It was like twenty years ago. I remember it well. She wore a uniform with marks of all different flavors of ice creams. I saw the play and came in to have a drink and a sandwich. There was this character sitting way down there, He was totally immersed in looking at this waitress. There was a commotion and I overheard someone taking bets on what was going to ensue. The stakes were quite high, close to fifty pounds a shot."

There was a big sigh from the audience.

"Yes, I am not exaggerating. The total pot was close to eight hundred and fifty pounds. Including my bet, it was nine hundred. I am proud to inform you that I won the bet. Everyone was predicting that Joanne would slap this bloke. There were others who'd had their faces slapped and some who lost their teeth."

Everyone laughed and some shouted, "Then what?" At least half of them were already tipsy with the amount of beer they had consumed. An unruly one wanted to know what she had done with the money.

"I was the only one who predicted that they would get married. They did get engaged on the same day, right there at that table where I was sitting. I was happy receiving 900 pounds of bet money. But more so for being especially invited to their wedding and having received their hospitality, friendship, love, and affection. Visiting them and meeting their lovely children and their friends, the doctors, was really a treat."

As she was saying these words, a huge cake was being pushed on a cart to the center. The whole audience was admiring the cake, which was at least five feet tall and four feet in diameter.

Mrs. Longworth continued. "The doctor friends couldn't make it to this celebration. They requested me to present this anniversary cake to John and Joanne and wish them a happy anniversary from every one of their friends in the United States."

John and Joanne were asked to cut the cake and the pieces were served to more than six hundred guests, basically the whole town.

The master of ceremonies came forward, took the mike, and said, "I don't wish to be a party pooper. But as you all know, many people and organizations have donated to this party. I have been co-coordinating the whole thing and I want to give a vote of thanks to some people and organizations."

There were claps from the audience.

"Our heartfelt thanks to the RSC for letting us use this venue for the party. Thanks to all the pub owners for this non-exhausting barrel of ale. Thanks to the Chamber of Commerce and local businesses for the beautiful posters and decorations. Last but not least, thanks to Dr. Rohit and Dr. Mamta, who have generously donated all the food and other expenses for the music and the lovely cake."

There were claps from the audience and all through the party photographs were being taken.

"Without much ado, I now present John and our own lovely Joanne."

John and Joanne came up the dais. There was clapping, whistling, and the singing of,

"For he's a jolly good fellow. She is a jolly good lady."

The clapping continued for at least three minutes. Many people there had known Joanne as she grew from a child, to a grown-up lady, and finally the mother of two children. They all loved her immensely. She reciprocated that individually and collectively. She was a remarkable person.

John took the mike and the crowd calmed down to hear him. "I just want to thank all of you for coming and of course our dear friends the doctors for everything. This is Joanne's day. She is an angel I stumbled upon in this restaurant. All I have been saying always is, 'Angel I love you. Angel I love you.' I better give this opportunity to the local gal and my dear wife, Joanne."

There was a thunderous clapping and everyone remarked on how much he loved her and how humble he was. The way the couple looked at each other spoke volumes. The Rao's had taken to them because they were an identical couple to themselves in the area of matrimonial bliss, though maybe Rohit was not as humble as John. He was a bit macho and often wanted his way. Mamta had wanted to attend this party very badly, but Rohit had already made plans for them to go to India.

In defense of Rohit, he was concerned that the old couple in India needed immediate medical attention. They were actually getting very depressed and in confidence had told Rohit the exact state of affairs. The grand old lady who'd raised Mamta had been diagnosed with cancer. The Indian doctors had given her only few months to live. She wanted to see the children and Mamta. Rohit did not want to tell that to Mamta because he knew how much she loved her grandparents and what effect it would have on her. So he was trying to ease the acceptance of the inevitable. This was a secret that Rohit had only shared with Joanne, since he knew how much Mamta liked Joanne. They were like twin sisters. This was a well-known fact even in Stratford. Every year Joanna and Mamta used to come to Stratford when there was a change of the play so they could catch two plays in one shot. Then they'd leisurely walk in the town square. All the shopkeepers knew them as the lovely Americans who bought expensive gifts for their friends in the USA. Once, Joanne had gone to India to meet the old couple. They got her to promise to take care of Mamta, since she was in a country that was not her motherland. When Joanne told them she was from England, they said that at least she was closer to the U.S.

The invitation for this party was as follows:

Mamta and Rohit Rao request the pleasure of your company with friends and relatives to celebrate the 20th wedding anniversary of their dear friends, Joanne and John, on Saturday June 22nd, 1985 starting at 8.00 p.m. through till dawn on Sunday June 23rd, 1985 or till the last person drops at whatever time on Sunday.

The bar is open and dinner buffet is open throughout
With best compliments:
RSC Staff and Restaurant Staff.
All businesses on the Town Square and Chamber of Commerce.

This was the first time an invitation came translated from an Indian language, word for word in England. Upon Joanne's insistence, a RSVP was attached. Mamta felt an RSVP did not reflect the hospitality that was usually expected in traditional Indian celebrations. The guests took the invitation literally and the whole town's RSVP was at their doorstep.

Mamta and Rohit did not mind the expense; they felt the friendship that they cherished was such that the monitory issue was trivial. Everyone at the party knew both Joanne and Mamta. When the news broke out that Mamta and Rohit were not going to be at the party, the whole town wondered why.

It was getting out of hand. Some said the two women had fought. It even went to the extent that there were said to be blows and punches thrown in between Mamta and Joanne. As if this did not have enough impact, they added some special Indian spice by dragging Rohit and John into the feud. For the Indian dessert they also involved the kids in the fight.

Actually, the town was having fun at the expense of these two families. I guess gossip and fabricated stories were part and parcel of the old British way. When Joanne got wind of what was happening, she wanted to cancel the party completely. It was Mamta who convinced her that it was OK for their friends to have some fun at their expense.

Joanne was furious every time she got a call from her close friend in Stratford. Finally she could not take it anymore and spilled the beans to her friend. Her friend took the opportunity to let everyone know why Mamta was not coming to the party and that it was because her grandmother had cancer and had been given only couple of months to live. She also explained that six weeks had elapsed and the old woman likely had only two weeks left.

Stratford suddenly experienced what it was like to be in a Shakespearean tragedy. It is easy for human beings to fabricate stories or rumors to have some fun, but they're usually started by insensitive people who lack self-esteem. The whole crowd there had been part of all this and felt pretty rotten for all the gossip, especially about people who were absolute darlings.

The crowd now chanted in unison, "Joanne…Joanne…Joanne."

This was like the cheer in Newcastle where they cheered their famous soccer players. Joanne took the mike and the clinking of the glasses started and wouldn't stop. She started her speech. "Guys if you know what's good for you, you'll stop right now. If he starts to kiss me it will be a long wait before I can say anything."

Even before she completed the sentence, John was holding her and kissing her passionately. The men in the crowd started to grab the gals next to them and took advantage and kissed them passionately. People heard some smacks, claps and slaps.

Joanne started again. "Guys."

In America "guys" often meant both genders. England being proper, the ladies in the crowd started to ask, "What about us gals?"

"OK, hey guys and gals."

There were claps from the crowd.

"We are all indebted to Mamta, my dear friend, for letting this party take shape the way it did. She is on her way to India to visit with her ailing grandmother. Don't we all wish she was here?"

"Yes, yes," the crowd answered.

"Their anniversary is coming pretty soon and…"

"We will give them a surprise party in the town square," the crowd answered. "It will be a surprise and the mayor said we will share everything. It will be like a festival in Stratford."

Joanne continued, "That will be a great party too; it will be a lot of fun. Both John and I want to thank all of you for attending this evening's celebrations. We will be having dancing pretty soon, to all the songs from the fifties and sixties."

The music started with "Tie a Yellow Ribbon Round the Ole Oak Tree," and as the opening few bars started, Joanne concluded by saying, "Have loads of fun, this isn't over till the last person drops."

The English know how to party. The beer flowed. People were getting tipsy and the party took on a life of its own. People migrated onto the lawns outside the glass wall and some did not even know whom they were with. They just felt as if they were part of royalty in the court of Henry and were smooching each other. Someone asked John and Joanne to join them on the lawns. There was a patch of square, tiled area where people could dance. When John and Joanne came onto the spot, their favorite song started to blast from the speakers. It was the hit that had been sung by The Cascades, "Rhythm of the Rain."

John took Joanne close to himself and started to dance. The whole crowd came to watch. As soon as the words "falling rain" came, as if by design, the automatic sprinklers kicked in and the crowd started cheering as Bob and Joanne danced with not a care in the world.

The songs started following one after other.

"You're just too good to be true. Can't take my eyes off of you…"

"Killing me softly with his song…"

"…Spanish eyes…"

"When the girl in your arms is the girl in your heart…"

"For I can't help falling in love with you…"

"Winter, spring, summer, or fall, all you have to do is call, and I will be there. You've got a friend…"

It was getting to be late at night. As a matter of fact, it was getting to be early dawn, around five a.m.

It was getting to be eleven p.m. in Cleveland. Rohit's SUV had just pulled into the driveway and he drove slowly to get to the car to the garage on the side of the house. The door had an opener and it started to open. Rohit drove his SUV in and out came his six-pack of beer, which had now become a four-pack, along with the packet of Kools and the lighter he'd reluctantly bought.

As he was coming into the house, Jose greeted him with, "How do you feel after the long drive, sir?"

"I am OK Jose. They are on their way."

"Do you want to eat anything?"

Mamta had gotten a promise from Jose that he would take care of Rohit while she was gone.

"I am going to watch *SNL* and go to bed. I have had my dinner."

" OK. I will get your breakfast ready in the morning."

"Make it a little late, say eight."

"Good night." So saying, Jose departed to his cottage, leaving Rohit alone to drink his forbidden beer and smoke his forbidden cigarettes.

The whole of Cleveland was sleeping except for few oddball old fellows like Jose's father, who could not sleep at nights. He was a perpetual TV watcher and was sitting in front of his TV watching a Spanish channel.

Jose walked in and seeing him said, "Why don't you sleep?"

"You know, and why do you ask me that every day?"

"I worry about you, Dad."

"I know, please don't worry…I am OK."

"Good night," said Jose and he went to bed.

The DJ was getting exhausted, but the guests were still going strong. The town started to wake-up. The birds started chirping in their nests. The swans that usually slept through the night with their long necks tucked away behind their backs underneath the feathers of their wings, started to pull them out and stretch them as if ready to go for another dance on the lawns of the RSC. The poor creatures had not had a peaceful wink all night.

There were couples intertwined under every tree, every bush, and every vine in the garden. Humans like to get drunk so their inhibitions leave them and they can systematically break the commandments. A wild party was an excuse, beer was a stimulus, and the mind went wild.

Humans usually don't realize that mind in itself is an intoxicated entity. All it requires is a push towards the realm of imagination. Usually it is a self-propelled entity and doesn't require any stimulus from outside. It was a perfect occasion for fun and frolic. Every imaginable fantasy was on the minds of the guests. The difference between the rich and the poor is that the rich preach to the poor and behave chastely for the perceivers. Once behind their walled compounds with shaded pines, their whims and fancies take very different turn, usually to an almost inexcusable ecstasy. The rich as usual come late to the party and leave early. They only have few sips of champagne and retire to their walled compounds for their own private party.

The commoners slowly get out of their misdoings with terrible hangovers. Often they are hand in hand with the wrong persons and once they realize what they have done they blame it on beer. They ask the brewer what witch's brew did he mix? In reality all of them know what they are doing. It is a perfect excuse.

The chaste see what is happening, and excuse themselves and convince themselves that the fault is in the witch's brew, while all along being curious what it would feel like to be naughty and mischievous. This is the funny thing about behavioral sciences. They don't question the restrictions placed on humans in the form of religion, social, civil, and royal commandments. What makes them right?

Everyone at the party except Joanne was happy that Mamta had not shown up. Mamta was pure and it would have been difficult for them to pull off their antics without feeling guilty. Why do we feel guilty when we see someone who is chaste? Why are we jealous and angry instead of being proud of knowing someone who is chaste? We are a complicated bunch of morons.

As the sun was coming out, there was a red hue that reflected off the dome of the theatre. It felt like there was blood dripping all over from the sky on all the people who were having indiscriminate fun. Why should people who did not suffer, be with those who did?

The kitchen was opened and few of the early shift workers went in to get ready to feed the waking battalion with hot coffee, fresh fruits, cereals, and western omelets. They had a TV in the kitchen to watch their favorite shows. All the guests were slowly coming into the hall to have their first early-morning coffee even without brushing their teeth. Some tried to show their conquests, usually the singles. Some tried to hide their imprudence under the guise of beer affliction. Some were feeling sorry for others. Some in particular were wondering what it would have been to be part of the group. But all were questioning *Why am I so inhibited about enjoying life?*

One of them caught something on the TV in the kitchen. They increased the volume to hear over the noise of the kitchen. All the kitchen staff was glued to the TV. There was a caption that said, "Breaking News." The time was 7.20. a.m.

"An Air India Jumbo 747 jet has crashed in the Irish Sea. The jet was heading from Montreal to New Delhi with a stopover in Heathrow. Unconfirmed reports indicate it might have been a terrorist attack. We will keep you informed of further developments...Now back to the scheduled programme."

The immediate response to the announcement was a strong reprimand from the head chef,

"Shut off that blasted television."

His assistant, who was the only person who could talk back to him, tried to explain but was asked to shut-up even before he'd completed his sentence.

Everyone went back to work preparing omelets for the crowd. Isn't it funny how people try to ignore or discard things they don't want to accept? They tend to push the dirt under the carpet. There was a definite queer feeling amongst all the kitchen staff. They did not know what to make of the ghastly announcement. They did not know if it was the flight Mamta was on. They just did not want to accept it. It was far easier for them to deny the facts. Question them? All the staff was mortally afraid of the head chef. They never questioned his decisions. The British hierarchy I suppose. However, in this case they all started to whisper to each other.

"Do you think that…?"

"Don't even say it. It is not."

"What if the news is untrue and it was not Air India?"

"How many times has the TV reported the wrong news?"

"They are never wrong."

"They get sued in America if they spread rumors."

"We have to be sure before we even tell anyone."

"Do you mean we are going to make this happy occasion into a cry session and spread gloom over every one?"

"No, not if we are unsure."

"So only if we are certain we should tell them."

"Tell whom?"

"John and Joanna."

"Who will tell them?"

"Not me."

"Not me."

"Not me."

The chef was listening to all the whispers. There was a silence in the kitchen that was unusual. There was not even the noise of the knife slicing through the vegetables being cut for the western omelets. But for the occasional sizzle of something falling on the hot grill, there was no sound. It looked like a morgue and not a kitchen. There were very many faces that were pale and lifeless. The chief was buying time, to think things over as to what would be his next step. He called his assistant and said, "Let's turn on the television and mute it. We shall follow the news on the captions. Everyone should act normal as if nothing has happened. Only when we have confirmed news and are sure that it is correct will we even venture to break the news."

"Shouldn't we confirm the flight she is on?"

"How will we do that?"

The youngest of the staff said, "They are still sitting on the bench outside. I will take some coffee out for them and casually find out the details."

Everyone felt it was a very good plan and started preparing a tray with a pot of coffee and two cups and saucers with cream and sugar and napkins with the pewter ring on them. It looked like there were two things that had not changed: pewter rings to hold napkins and friends to console bereavement.

The young waitress slowly walked through the lawns to where John and Joanne were sitting and placed the tray on the picnic table beside the bench. In a very pleasant voice she said, "Good morning."

I guess everyone in Stratford is an accomplished actress. She did not let her anxiety show. She was her natural self. She was so pleasant that anyone who was with her would like to have talked to her.

"Good morning. Did you have fun last night?" said Joanne with a warm smile.

"Yes mum, I did but had to cut it short since I had morning shift duty."

"I used to do the morning shift also, since I never partied much."

"Mum, yesterday I heard you talk about your friend." She started the conversation as she was pouring coffee into the cups, and she continued, "Do you take cream and sugar, sir?"

"Please. One spoon of sugar and a dash of cream."

"Same for me," Joanne said.

The waitress again continued the topic of Mamta, making sure not to give any hints of anxiety. "She is a close friend of yours isn't she?"

Joanne always wanted to talk about Mamta. "I miss her. She wanted to come to this party very badly."

"Why didn't she?"

"Her grandma is on her deathbed and has only few days to live."

"Oh no!"

"She is on her way to India; actually she might be right above us."

This was a comment the young girl did not expect. Her face suddenly turned pale and for a moment she lost her composure. Acting on the stage may be different from acting in real life. We all wear masks. We are not what we are perceived to be. We are animals of what we please and put up a front for what we want to be perceived as. She recovered fast. She was a true thespian. "Is she flying Air Canada?"

"No, she is flying Air India."

"I thought she was flying from…" She paused to give Joanne a chance to fill in the blanks.

Joanne fell for it. "Montreal."

"Oh no!" she blurted.

"What?"

"I left the freezer door open when I took the cream."

"Oops. The chef won't tolerate that."

"I better head back, mum." Having accomplished her task, she ran back to the kitchen. There were tears streaking down her rosy cheeks. She was young and couldn't control herself. As she got closer to the kitchen, she started to cry. She wiped her face with the apron she was wearing and all the makeup that had been on her face now adorned her apron. Some of the guests who were already seated in the main restaurant were perturbed by what they saw. This was like a wrong note in a romantic symphony being performed by the London Symphony Orchestra.

Joanne and John felt something was not right. Joanne always comforted people who were in distress. "An open freezer door?" she wondered. She knew it was something beyond an open freezer door and she started to instant-replay her conversation with the girl. She also remembered that when she'd commented about Mamta being above them, the girl had turned pale as if she'd seen a ghost. Joanne guessed that there was something wrong in the kitchen and that it had to do with either her or Mamta. She did not waste any time asking John to follow; she ran towards the kitchen. John followed her, forgetting that he was holding onto the napkin on the tray. The tray came trashing down onto the cement floor. The expensive Royal Dolton china shattered into many pieces. The coffee pot broke and spilled all over.

The black color of the coffee and the splattered coffee grinds indicated gloom and doom.

As she was running up the stairs, the waitress slipped, fell, and hit her face on the top step. Her face got cut in a few places and blood started to gush. Joanne and John were catching up with her. She got up and headed towards the kitchen with them only a step behind. Seeing the commotion, all the inebriated guests sobered up and followed the procession into the kitchen. As the waitress entered the kitchen with her blood-splattered face, not even caring about her injuries, every one figured there was something amiss. She screamed out loud, "It's her plane that crashed…It's her plane that crashed…she is dead…she is dead…Mamta is dead."

There was a sudden calm and silence in the place. Everyone's eyes now focused on Joanne. The poor girl turned around and found herself suddenly facing Joanne.

They stared at each other for a moment. Joanne couldn't believe what she'd heard. Her eyes and expression were asking innumerable questions as to what this young woman was babbling about Mamta. The waitress suddenly broke the silence with a big sob, and walking towards Joanne she said, "The Air India flight carrying Mamta crashed in the northern Irish Sea."

As if by design, the TV was taken off mute—really, it took itself off mute. How did it happen? In any case, it facilitated the explanation of something for which no one there had enough details.

"The latest reports indicate that there were no survivors in the early morning crash of the Air India flight from Montreal. A terrorist attack is suspected. We will keep you informed as further information is available."

Everyone there was stunned into silence. They all worried about Joanne's reaction. John was beside her. She just closed her eyes, fell into his arms, and swooned. John held her close and said, "It's God's way of comforting people who are in trauma. Let's let it take its course."

The news had hit the United Kingdom first. There was a piece of aluminum fuselage floating in the Irish Sea with a name on it: "Emperor Kanishka." It is said he was one of the early, peace-loving emperors of the Indian Sub-Continent.

Chapter Twelve

It was few minutes before eleven when Rohit bid goodnight to Jose. He set his beer on the center island in the kitchen, took one bottle, opened it, and slowly started to trek up the stairs. There was complete silence in the mansion. Other than the sounds of crickets and bull frogs on the shores of Lake Erie, there was absolutely still silence with the exception of Mamta's waterfall. All in all, it was very peaceful. The grandfather clock in the main family room was keeping beat with Rohit's heartbeat. He was an athlete and ran five miles every morning. His heartbeat was sixty and there were sixty seconds in a minute. So the clock and the heart were trying to establish who was going to be the first to miss a beat.

The grandfather clock had two chimes programmed into it. There were the London Big Ben or the Westminster Abbey chimes as options. The abbey was not only a church but it was also the resting place for royalty. This was the reason that Mamta always wanted the clock to be set to the Big Ben chime. When Jose's father was dusting that afternoon, he'd inadvertently pushed the lever to the Westminster chime.

Rohit was climbing the stairs and as he reached the top, the eleven o'clock chimes started to ring the Westminster Abbey melody. He stopped for a minute and felt uneasy at hearing the chime that was disliked by Mamta. If Mamta had been there he would have gone down and fixed it. But this was his freedom time and he shrugged and said out loud, "You can chime all you want till morning."

The stairs entered a loft area at the top. It had decorative railing all around where it was open to the ground floor. There were three doors into the loft area. They all were double doors with exquisite carvings made out of rosewood imported from India. Monty Hall would have loved to have these for Doors One, Two, and Three on his show, *Let's make a Deal.*

It's funny that we always make deals with God. But He dishes out deals that are what you expected—some times less than and sometimes more than what you expected. When He gets up on the wrong side of the bed, he dishes out something completely contrary to what you expected. It's like fighting Muhammad Ali in a dark ring; you don't know when the punch will land and that's it.

The double door to the north side of the house entered the master bedroom. It opened to the north with a spectacular view of Lake Erie. It was from this vantage point that sometimes Mamta and Rohit sat side by side on the rocker, cuddled-up together to see God's theatre. Mamta always used to comment about how peaceful the lake waters were and that they did not know what lay ahead for them. She was commenting on the huge thunderous drop they would experience as they freefell the height of Niagara Falls. As usual, Rohit had to have the final say; he used to remind her that not all the water went over the falls and that there was a lot of water that flowed through the power station. Mamta actually was smarter than Rohit. She countered by saying, yes these waters had a greater trauma than the Niagara waters. At least God orchestrated Niagara whereas the powerhouse had been built by some engineer to satisfy the insatiable thirst for energy. She reminisced that even though they did not have electricity when she was growing up in the village with her grandfather and grandmother, they still had a lot of fun and that she would rather have been there than in the fully-lit towns.

The rocker was on an open terrace flanking the bedroom. On occasion John and Joanne used to join them and they all enjoyed the best view of Lake Erie in Cleveland.

The other two doors opened to the south side and were Sunny and Seshi's bedrooms. Rohit made sure that the doors to his kids' rooms were properly closed. He opened his bedroom door, walked in, switched on the lamp besides the bed, and walked onto the terrace. From there he could see the lakeside cottage. Jose Sr. was watching his television, and the blue hue could be seen from the window.

Time is an entity with its own mind, whereas the mind has many misgivings about time. You really don't know how it is that time passes by quickly when you are having fun and goes slowly when you are alone. Does it really speed up and slow down? Time is man-made and so is God. Time has no relevance when you are in outer space. Our measurement of time is based on what we perceive as the totality. When we try to put it in terms of the universe it just fails miserably.

The minutes were long, the seconds were long, and there was an uneasiness in Rohit. Perhaps it was his freedom binge and he was feeling guilty about what he had been up to. Still feeling guilty, he pulled a Kool from his pack and lit it. He took a deep puff, pulled some more fresh air into his mouth, and then after few seconds exhaled a big puff of smoke. He placed his cigarette between his lips and using his two hands opened the beer bottle. He threw the bottle cap as hard as he could to try and reach the water of the lake. It didn't reach. He held his cigarette in his left hand and his beer in his right.

He looked at the rocker that was standing still on the terrace. There was not a blade of grass nor a leaf on the trees moving. The smoke from his cigarette hovered right above his head as if it did not know what else to do. It was like the fog described by Arthur Conan Doyle in the story, "The Hound of the Baskervilles." The lake was calm and absolutely serene.

Jose was in his bed but didn't feel sleepy and tossed from side to side. He saw Rohit standing on the terrace, smoking and drinking his beer. Jose thought about the promise he'd made to Mamta that he would take care of Rohit. He wondered how he could reinforce her ethics in him? Should Rohit have the freedom to do what he wanted, or would the institution of marriage take that right away from him? Why did Mamta insist that he take care of himself, to what end? She was a very secure person in her own right. She didn't need his financial backing to live. Then why did she do it? She didn't want him to go before her, I mean to the Gates of Heaven. Jose was trying to put some logic behind the female demands on the male species. Every time he saw Mamta, he wanted to marry. But when the thought came that his chosen lady might not have Mamta's disposition, he quickly backed out of the possibility of marrying anyone and being disappointed that she didn't match his expectations. As long as Mamta was around, Jose would probably never get married.

With all these crazy thoughts flashing through his mind, through his window he took a glimpse at Rohit on the terrace. His window had bars on it. It was to protect the fishing equipment left unattended in the beach house. For a minute Jose saw Rohit as if he were behind bars in a prison. The bars had a very deep connotation.

Aren't we all behind bars of some sort? Bars placed by religion. Bars placed by friends. Bars placed by spouses. Bars placed by children. Bars placed by society. Bars placed by government, other countries, other religious heads, other counter-thinkers. Bars placed by God.

Who is God? Who made Him? Is He a man or women? Anything which is man-made is not an absolute truth. We are all prisoners of the bodies we live in. We are all prisoners of our beliefs. We are all prisoners of each other's wrath because of dogmatic, irrelevant beliefs.

Many believe that zero is perfect. If it is perfect, explain to me why we have 32 degree Centigrade equal to 0 degrees Fahrenheit. Zero is imperfect. Is birth perfect? No way it is. It discriminates between the sexes. Often, the male unit is dominant and the female unit is subservient. It lets some be born in poor Biafra and some in the rich USA.

It's only death that is perfect. It does not discriminate between sexes, race, ethnicity, citizenship, color, or religion.

It was funny that Jose Sr. also got up from his Lazy Boy, saw Rohit on the terrace, and had similar sentiments reeling through his brain.

The night has a very strict schedule. It wears people down. Whether you like it or not, it puts you to sleep. Jose started to yawn and soon sleep took over his senses and he was out like a light. Rohit finished his cigarette and beer and went in and lay in his bed. His thoughts went to the small village in India. He was afraid as to how Mamta would react to the news that her grandmother was in her last days waiting for the inevitable. Cancer has no sympathy does it? Sleep overcame him also and he slowly got to the snore level of sleep. Three things only disturbed the stillness and silence: Jose's Mexican snore, Rohit's Indian snore, and the sound of the Mexican TV station.

The grandfather clock started its duty by chiming the quarter notes of the Westminster Abbey chime. As if there was some commotion, all the birds in the area started to chirp away. It was not in the usual, soft, early-morning style but as if there were a snake coming close to their nest and their chicks. Jose Sr. felt there was some evil lurking around and came out of the beach house to investigate. The still water in the lake started to get agitated.

Slowly, the waves started to pick up. It was a very unusual event. There was no wind whatsoever. Still there were waves that were close to ten to fifteen feet. He stood on the wooden boat ramp. The waves started to approach the ramp where the boat Rohit had christened *Mamta* was moored. The waves approached closer to the coastline. Jose Sr. was completely convinced that something was happening that was not ordinary. The waves approached the boat. Jose Sr. stood face to face with this fifteen-foot wave. He, with his tiny build, looked like a dwarf compared to the wave that was approaching. Within seconds it picked up the boat and it rode on the crest of the wave. As if by specific intent, the wave tossed the boat about forty feet into the air and into the middle of the lake. Jose Sr. stood there, staring at the boat, which took flight with the rope following it, dragging the anchor. It was as if the anchor wasn't worth a goddamn cent.

The grandfather clock labored to tick seconds and minutes. The minutes were like hours. Suddenly, as if all the canine battalion had woken up, the dogs in the neighborhood started to howl like wolves. Jose Sr. stood there, speechless. The wave hit the shore and he was completely drenched. The water temperature was unusually cold and frigid for that time of the year. All the stars were twinkling bright as if asking, what was the matter? The boat landed upside down on the water. The grandfather clock indicated that only five minutes had passed since it chimed for quarter past the hour of twelve.

The boat landed squarely on the water and ensued a big bang. The sound was deafening. One wondered if they were in Hiroshima, or Pearl Harbor. The boat was shattered into pieces and there was a piece of the stern with the name *Mamta* floating in the rough waters. The sound shook the house and the boathouse.

All the commotion woke Rohit, Jose, and his mother. Jose's mother came running out. Finding Jose Sr. not perched in front of the television but out on the boat ramp, drenched, she screamed. The fury of the lake had not abated but was continuing to escalate. Rohit came onto the terrace, wondering what was happening. Looking at the high waves he shouted, "It looks like a storm will come into the house! Abandon the lake house!" The minute his voice hit the area there was a kind of soothing amidst the chaos.

Jose replied, " It's OK. If it gets bad we will come in."

It looked as though the rain had decided to join in the fun. Rohit went in and locked the terrace door behind him.

Jose Sr. asked, "Jose, you did not tell him about the boat?"

"What boat, Dad?" enquired Jose.

Jose Sr. could only point to the dock where had been moored. His wife was literally pulling him inside.

Rohit got back into his bed and got ready to get back to his sleep.

Jose realized what had happened to the boat and said, "What can he do now? Let's tell him tomorrow."

The fury of the lake was still on and it looked as though it was quite angry at something or someone.

For some unknown reason, Jose and his parents felt comforted when a red streak of light came close to them, as if to assure them that everything would be OK. The streak moved on to the lake and as if by magic, the lake calmed down completely without making a ripple. It lay there like a sheet of glass reflecting its surroundings.

A blue streak of light and a white one appeared. They went on to the terrace and hovered there as if to get permission from the red streak of light. Rohit had locked the doors because he did not want them to rattle in the wind. The red streak, after hovering on the lake, joined the other two on the terrace. This spooked the three onlookers below and they quickly went into the cottage and locked the door behind them.

Jose went to bed, his dad back to the TV after a change of clothes, and his mom went into the kitchen to make a hot cup of tea for the old man.

The three streaks hovered on the terrace for a moment and the red streak moved to the locked door. The door opened by itself. There was an unusual breeze that entered the master bedroom. The drapes started to float in the breeze. The noise of the door opening awakened Rohit. He saw the three bright lights. He was not scared. He felt he had a connection with the three. The double doors leading into the loft opened. The white glow and the blue glow moved through the door and each opened the children's bedroom doors. The white entered Sunny's room and the blue entered Seshi's room.

Rohit was perplexed. He knew whatever they were, they were trying to communicate. He heard a big noise from Seshi's room and proceeded to investigate. A favorite picture of Seshi was down on the floor with the glass shattered. Rohit saw the blue glow grow bright and slowly fade away as he approached the picture, lifted it, and turned it over. It was the picture taken on the day Seshi had been accepted into medical school. She was proud and she had taken a picture with her father, who was proud of his daughter. Rohit placed the picture on the bed. He felt uneasy.

He proceeded to Sunny's room to find the white glow was still bright. It was on the bed, hovering, before it slowly began to fade. On the bed, Rohit found the Father's Day card that Sunny had given him that year. As he picked up the card and read its inscription, the glow faded out. All the card said was, "I love you, Dad."

Suddenly there were tears in Rohit's eyes. Something felt wrong. He ran back into his room to find the red glow.

The red glow was on the bed where Mamta used to sleep. As he approached the bed and sat, the glow moved away and perched itself on the rocking chair beside the window where Mamta always used to sit. The rocking chair started to rock exactly the same way it would when Mamta sat on it. The glow moved onto the terrace and when it reached the double rocker, it hovered on it for a moment and then faded.

Rohit did not know what to make of the whole thing. He sat on the double rocker and lit a cigarette.

The lake was back to normal; everything was calm just as it had been when he'd come home from Toronto. He wondered how in just ten minutes the whole storm and all the events had happened.

Mustering enough courage, Jose came out and addressed Rohit. "Are you OK, Doctor, sir?"

Rohit answered that he was. He finished his cigarette and went back to bed, this time not locking the doors. It didn't seem to matter if they were locked or not.

Jose went back to his sleep. As he was trying to get a wink of sleep, Rohit struggled to understand the meaning of the events that had just occurred. In the cottage, Jose's mom muttered that she did not like the omens as she gave her husband the tea and went to bed. The insomniac sat in his favorite LazyBoy and watched his Spanish TV.

The grandfather clock chimed the half-hour chime. The local time was thirty minutes after midnight.

PG's audience was getting tense. Priya was excited at the opportunity to helm a production of the caliber that she was listening to. Simrin was happy to have been promoted, but was teary-eyed as she listened to PG's heart-wrenching rendition of the story.

They felt they needed a break. Priya said, "PG, how about continuing tomorrow?"

There was no resistance from any one and the meeting was adjourned.

No one wanted to miss anything that was going to follow. Next day, they were all in the office early, waiting for PG to show. He dragged his weary, shabby sack of skin loaded with bones and flesh and a forlorn heavy heart. He looked as if he had not gotten any sleep the previous night.

Bob, as usual, had come early and climbed up the stairs. When he'd reached his floor, he was completely drenched in sweat. He'd had his quick shower and gotten dressed in a Polo shirt and olive-green pants. He had started to respect PG for his story and the way the characters were playing. He felt it was like the old master, Pirandello, back, writing another one of his plays.

A late-August sun was too weary to get up and get going. New York, as usual, was full of life. Everyone was getting ready for the long weekend before school started. Priya's count of admirers was down to fewer than five. The construction was completed and there were not too many people on the streets.

Seeing PG in that shape, a concerned Simrin asked, "Are you OK?."

"It's sometimes difficult for an author to distinguish between fact and fiction."

"Especially when the characters are near and dear," she said.

If it had been anyone else, he would have bitten their head off, but he had developed a special rapport with Simrin and that was the saving grace.

Simrin quickly understood what she had said. Sometimes we say things that are true, though all along, the listener wants to forget them…to push them into the deep depths of the crevices in his brain.

"A good author usually fathers his characters and molds them to his utopian standard. Doesn't he?" she asked.

"They were my friends. Fiction is an exaggeration of truth."

Everyone had their plans for the long weekend and in more than one way, everyone wanted this interesting story to come to its conclusion before they took off for their break.

PG cleared his throat and got on his soapbox.

It is said that devout Hindus like Mamta can sense death approaching. They believe that they are entwined in a cycle of birth and death. They also believe that there exists within them and all humans a divine soul. This divinity is not affected by *Samsara*, which is the cycle of death and rebirth. It's only the body complex with the five senses, that is affected. The five senses are the four horses and the charioteer, guiding them through this *Maya*, which is an illusory manifestation.

In this belief the body becomes an essential factor for the soul. Hindus believe that the soul is subjected to the bondage of the body in living from birth to death. They believe that the body continues to live for a period of fourteen days even after the soul has departed, during which they try to calm the soul and guide it to depart from the *Samsara*. The inactive body is not allowed to continue and is cremated, within twenty-four hours. The soul lingers around the bondages of *Samsara* and its loved ones. Based on their karma (intentional actions and their results) some souls linger around their dear ones before either merging with the divine soul *Moksha* or finding another place to be reborn according to their destiny.

Chapter Thirteen

Sometimes insomniacs do have moments when they dose off. One such moment presented itself for Jose Sr. that night at one-twenty a.m. The Spanish TV station got wind of the air disaster and aired a breaking news segment. The insomniac slept through the first broadcast. Television news executives, for some odd reason, want to be the first to let the world know what a rotten species we are. Under the guise of it being a human-interest story they want to drill into our ears and eyes any news they feel is worthy or has sensationalism.

During the Second World War and after, in the small village of Bobbar Lanka, in Andhra Pradesh, where Mamta grew-up with her grandparents, there used to be what they called touring talkies. This was like a circus tent that went from place to place and showed 35 mm movies. The storylines were escapist avenues for the layman to forget his daily trials and tribulations in earning a livelihood. Talkies meant movies with sound. On a Sunday night they had special showings of English movies. That was the night all the so-called elite of the village went to watch. There were Technicolor movies like *Samson and Delilah* with Victor Mature and Hedy Lamar. That one won Oscars for best costumes and production design.

Mamta's grandfather, who was a painter, used to comment on movie color consultant Leonard Doss's excellent color compositions. These shows were a substitute for Viagra, with their vivacious leading ladies. You know what I mean.

It was there that they used to hear and see news on the *Metro World News*, which ran for twelve minutes. It gave all the news with pictures. Often, news like the attack on Pearl Harbor reached these touring talkies two to three weeks after the event had occurred.

As Jose Sr. dozed, the Spanish-language station started to pound the TV with the breaking news between every commercial break. The clock on the wall gonged twice, suggesting it was 1.30 a.m. and the breaking news item being was rerun. The sound of the gong woke up Jose Sr., so he saw the news item. But this had been his only opportunity to pick-up on a wink of sleep and he dozed off again. Suddenly, he woke-up and slowly, without making much noise, he walked up to his son's room.

Jose hadn't gotten much sleep the night before as he'd been cleaning the carpet, washing the clothes, packing the bags, and preparing the breakfast. He was snoring. Jose Sr. did not know whether to wake him or not. He sat on the bed, and looked at his son, and whispered, *"Hijo, algo muy malo."*[6]

Jose did not react. His father put his hands on him and shook him.

Jose's sleep was disturbed and he opened his eyes and saw his dad. His first and foremost worry was his father's health and he surmised that most probably Jose Sr. wasn't feeling good. His greatest fear was that his father might leave him and go far away into the stars. "What Dad? Are you OK?"

"Ishhh. Don't wake Mom."

"What?"

"Come with me."

"Where?" Jose got out of bed and followed his dad to the TV room. As he walked in he saw the news broadcast. His eyes filled with tears, which slowly started to streak down.

His father had been maintaining his composure till then, but now he also had a few tears in his eyes. Old people get accustomed to being able to handle this kind of news. Age has something to do with it. They have been drilled through these kinds of things off and on. So they understand that some issues of human evolution are such that they have to have a full stop. All commas, semi-colons, whatever they are, have a full stop at the end.

Jose's silent tears slowly turned into sobs. He hugged his father and cried out loud. Hearing the commotion, his mom came out of the bedroom. When Jose saw his mom he bawled out and hugged her. She was his security

---

6 Son, something very bad.

blanket from his childhood. Both his parents comforted him. No one could say anything in a situation like this where they didn't know what to do.

"We got to wake-up Doctor Sir," Jose Sr. said.

"Can't it wait till morning?" Jose said, crying out loud.

"Not if he has to make arrangements to go."

"I cannot tell him," The denial had started to set in. "What if they are OK and we get him all worked-up?"

"Son, listen to me, you have got to wake him and ask him to watch CNN news. Let him make his own decisions."

"I don't want to tell him."

Jose Sr. was stern. "Jose, tell him to watch CNN."

Jose had no choice. He continued to cry out loud.

"It's OK to cry…it's OK to cry," his mom assured him. She was listening all along and had tears in her eyes, but as all mothers do, she tried to put up a strong front for her son. After he went out of the cottage, she saw her husband and broke down completely.

Jose started to head off to the main building. He was still crying and mumbling to himself. "Why did I pack their bags? I should have just let them alone. Maybe then they might have postponed for a day. Why do things happen like this to good people? The airline companies should take care of their planes better."

Still crying, he opened the back door climbed the stairs, and entered the bedroom. He approached the bed.

The crying disturbed Rohit's sleep. He got up and saw Jose sobbing. His immediate reaction was that something had happened to Jose Sr. He knew how paranoid Jose was about his father, and how much he loved him. "Jose, is Dad OK?"

"CNN." Still crying, Jose couldn't say much more.

Rohit, for once in his life, tried to comfort someone by putting his arm around him and he walked with Jose to the kitchen. "It will be OK. Trust me. It will be OK, whatever it is."

Rohit looked for the remote and Jose found it and gave it to him. Rohit turned the TV on and tuned it to CNN. It was commercial time and they had to wait two minutes for the ads to run through. Rohit picked up a beer, opened it at the center island of the kitchen, and started to sip.

"Now back to breaking news."

CNN started repeating the news. Jose stared at Rohit, watching his countenance change. Rohit's face paled. His demeanor become aggravated and agitated. In matter of seconds the past two weeks rolled before him like a Charlie Chaplin walk, fast, furious, silent, and into the far horizon.

He was still at the center island in the kitchen. Jose was frightened. He'd never seen his employer's face change to that furious state. Quickly, he moved to the steps and sat on them away from Rohit. He looked at Rohit through the railings, feeling as if he were in a prison with bars around him of love, affection, and companionship.

Rohit remembered the long-distance call from Mamta's grandfather, Bobber Lanka. The old man had been literally crying on the phone and wanted to know if Mamta was around. Finding that she was out with her friend Joanne, planning the anniversary party, he started to talk freely. He explained that Mamta's grandmother was very sick. The cancer had taken a quick turn. Doctors gave her only few days of life, at most a week to ten days. He asked Rohit to send Mamta and the kids under the guise of celebrating Seshi's forthcoming birthday.

Mamta had already bought her tickets to go to the UK and spend time with her dear friend Joanne. Much against her wishes, Rohit had to cancel her trip to UK and literally force her to take the kids to take this trip to India. He remembered Mamta saying, "The die is cast," and recalled her comment when the sheriff's assistant was sent to get them out of the traffic jam. "Evil often takes advantage of good."

He knew that Mamta had been hoping that they would miss the flight. She never expressed herself firmly and was always ready to compromise. That was a trait of all Indian women and men often took advantage of it as a weakness. Rohit was not taking advantage but in his own way had been trying to facilitate her grandfather's wishes. He felt guilty sending her to India when Joanne was celebrating her anniversary. So his only redemption was to confide the real truth to Joanne. The whole thing had just taken the matter of one nano-second.

The CNN newsbreak explained the situation in exacting terms.

The thought of his family's plight was reinforced. The beer in his hand tasted like poison. He threw the beer bottle at the TV in disgust. It missed the TV, went through the window, and fell at the feet of Jose Sr., who was approaching the house. The old man understood that the news had reached Rohit and he turned back to the cottage. Jose sat at the foot of the steps, still looking at Rohit through the railings. He felt he was a prisoner now, since he'd promised Mamta to take care of Rohit. This would now be a job till the end of his life or to the end Rohit's life, whichever came first. In his fury, Rohit threw all the rest of the beer bottles and broken glass scattered all over.

The TV started to give the news again. "News on the hour every hour."

Rohit walked towards the TV. There was broken glass all over and he was barefoot. He came within five feet of the TV. The news sank in and he realized that he'd lost all his family. His eyes filled with tears. Searching for comfort, he looked around for Jose and spotted him sitting on the stairs behind the railings.

Jose looked at him.

"Jose…Jose…Did you hear what they are saying?" His voice was gruff and trembling. "Jose… Jose…" He could not continue.

Jose got up and slowly walked to him. His shoes crackled the broken glass on the tile floor. He approached his boss. Grief knows no barriers; it does not know any religion, it does not know color, it does not know ethnicity, and it does not have artificiality associated with it. No pride can stop it. No prejudice can conquer it. It engulfs one's total self and only allows one to search for solace. That's how the original concept of God came along, as the psychological solace for people who were downtrodden. Sometimes the oppressed and the oppressor pray to the same God.

Rohit didn't feel the pain of all the glass that had cut his feet. They were bleeding profusely. Jose saw the blood and the cuts and could not bear it. He started to feel that he was not keeping up his promise to Mamta. As he came close, Rohit just stared at him and Jose stared back. Neither knew what to say or what to do.

"Jose, are you thinking what I am thinking?"

Jose was lost as how to answer that question. Should he just ignore the facts and say everything was all right? The only thing he could do was bawl out loud. Rohit took him close, and using his shoulder, started to cry out loud as well. The two were crying so loudly their plight was heard at the cottage. Jose's mother could not bear her son's crying. She wanted to get to the mansion. Jose Sr. stopped her and said that they needed that private time before the whole world started to come.

Jose remembered his promise, led his boss to the Lazy Boy seat in front of the TV, and made him sit there. He asked him not to move around while he got the vacuum and picked up the glass pieces lest he stepped on them again. He brought some antibiotic ointment and some cotton gauze and removes all the glass pieces from Rohit's feet, then he administered the ointment and bandaged his feet. He bought him his house slippers to wear.

As this first-aid work went on, Rohit stared at the guest room, which had a Red Cross sign on it. This was called the sick room. Any guests Mamta invited were usually sick people she was caring for, who had neither the insurance coverage nor the means to pay obnoxious doctor bills.

Rohit remembered when he was very sick and was admitted to this residential Mamta Free Clinic. He was so sick he was unable to take his medicine on time. So Mamta said they would set an alarm clock to remind them that it was time for his medicine.

He was sleeping under the influence of the sleeping tablet given to him to ease the pain. Suddenly, someone shook him and said, "Time for the medicine, dear."

Rohit was so drugged that all he did was get up with Mamta's help and swallow the pills. As soon as the two pills found their way into his stomach, the alarm sounded. Mamta was quick to shut it off it because was late at night—to be exact, it was two a.m. He commented, "How do you do that? Even beat the alarm clock?"

Her words still rang in his ears, as he wept aloud to Jose, "She said that I was everything to her. She said I protect her and take care of her. She said that she prays to God that I should live long and that he…" Sobs overwhelmed him and he couldn't proceed any further.

It was Jose's turn. "She was like that a Florence Nightingale."

"Yes, she said she wanted God to take her before me. I forced her to go. I should have let her postpone till after Joanne's party."

"No, it was my fault. I called the sheriff's office to help you to get beyond that bad accident. Otherwise she would have missed the plane."

"Jose, take me upstairs to my room for few hours. I want to be there alone," requested Rohit.

Jose helped him up to his bedroom and once he was on his bed, pulled up a blanket and put it on him. Rohit tried to prop himself up and Jose organized some pillows to get him comfortable. Finally, he said, "I will be downstairs. Call me if you need anything."

Jose left the room still crying, leaving Rohit crying and coughing with a very heavy heart. Down in the kitchen, Jose started to clean the blood on the floor. His mother couldn't wait any longer and came to comfort her son. Jose said, "He is alone Mama, he doesn't have anyone to take care of him."

It was a profound statement. That's the reality that hits the first-generation immigrants. They lose their parents and their near and dear in the good old country, be it the UK, Germany, Italy, Mexico, India, or any other country. They find that it becomes hard to take grief. Rohit, an only son, Mamta an only daughter; both were each other's friends and confidants.

Rohit sat in his bed and started to reminisce about the good times they'd shared together and with their children. As if Mamta had not left, the rocking chair near the window rocked in the wind that blew in from Lake Erie. It looked as if it had orders from his beloved to comfort Rohit. Surges of grief overcame Rohit, with lulls in between.

The night was taking its toll on everyone who was close to that family, but the commotion had not yet hit Cleveland in these early hours. Cleveland still slept, unaware of what has happened.

India too was still ignorant of this new event in the complicated world we live and interact with.

The world had just witnessed one of its earliest terrorist attacks.

In ancient India, battles were fought on some basic principles. They started at sunrise and stopped at dusk. The mighty proved their strength under the watchful eyes of God. The participants did not know what an ambush was, or a preemptive attack.

A new era had begun…

Chapter Fourteen

The Westminster Abbey chime from the grandfather clock indicated that it was three o'clock in the morning.

Cleveland slept like a baby. Euclid Avenue was barren and lifeless. There was only the odd police cruiser driving around, making sure there were no vandals taking advantage of the night silence.

The chief resident at Cleveland Christian General Hospital was having an easy night. He went to the walk-in linen closet and started to get a few winks. Debbie, the ER nurse, had been given instructions to wake him up if an emergency arose. Usually the weekend was bad news. They had all kinds of patients: some with knife wounds from bar brawls; gunshot wounds from the coke dealers, and predominantly, injuries from motorcycle accidents. For some reason, car drivers fail to see motorcyclists, perhaps because they are not as visible as cars.

But the calm that night was broken with a unique situation. A truckload of patients was brought in. Everyone was completely blood soaked, with their throats slashed, stab wounds in their chests, or smashed faces. In spite of all their injuries, these hardy people were all walking around on their own steam. Some older nurses freaked. Younger ones stood their ground.

The Code Blue was put out on the speaker and all the residents and doctors on call flocked to the ER. The whole hospital was ready to take care of the injured.

The chief resident started to take notes to admit the injured, only to find that they all were actors and actresses from an indie movie being shot in Cleveland. As they had been shooting on a horrifying schedule, a raised platform on the set suddenly collapsed and all the actors had fallen from a height of four feet. The producer of the flick wanted to make sure that no one was badly hurt. He was actually preempting any suits against his company. None of these actors were being paid; they were doing it for the sake of art and to see their name as the titles rolled at the end of the flick. Initially everyone at the hospital was worried, but when they found out the truth they had a laugh.

The ER nurse, Debbie glanced at the TV and came across the news of the Air India crash. The assistant-sheriff, as usual, came in to get a free coffee as well as a tête á tête with his fiancée, Debbie. Debbie casually mentioned to him about the crash. Police have very high IQs and he immediately figured out what it meant. He alerted Debbie to the possibility of Dr. Mamta Rao being on that flight. A horrified Debbie informed the chief resident, who asked her to inform the administrator immediately. The assistant-sheriff called the sheriff and woke him up from his bed. Time was moving very stealthily. It looked as if it did not want to move ahead and let people know of what had happened to Dr. Mamta Rao. Time felt as if people did not know it might happen. It wanted to be like Clark Kent—to make the world go backwards for a day and maybe save Mamta. It is such an irony that time has the capacity to heal all wounds, but on the other hand is helpless in being the architect of events and happenings.

Rohit sat on his bed. The white drapes fluttered in the breeze. Heavy, red-velvet drapes adorned the big bay windows. On either side were thick ropes hanging from the top. They were brown in color and looked like king cobras hanging from the curtain rods.

Many a Westerner often talks about the Indian rope trick. It is a simple illusion in the way of Sherlock Holmes' "Elementary, my dear Watson." There is in Indian philosophy a treatise on *Rajue*, which means a jute rope. The philosophy explains that when one sees a coiled jute rope in a corner of a dark room, one can mistake it for a king cobra. Our minds are pre-programmed to perceive things first as a danger and then to discard the fear upon investigation. Now when the perceiver lights up the room, he realizes it is only a *Rajue*-jute rope. His ignorance has been removed and he is enlightened to the actual truth—that the coiled entity at the corner is not really a king cobra but merely a harmless rope.

Maya is the veils of ignorance. Just as a light establishes the misconception of the rope being a snake, one should enlighten one's thought process to peel away the layers of ignorance. Knowledge is omnipresent and omnipotent. It is only understood as one develops and removes the veils of *Maya*.

Did apples refuse to fall on the ground till Newton expounded the theory of gravity?

Rohit was just staying in his room as Jose watched closely to be there if he needed him.

The administrator arrived at the hospital as the morning sun was peeping through. Debbie informed him of the sad news. He immediately asked the custodian to bring the flags in the front to half-mast. He then started to make arrangements to issue a memorandum to the effect that Dr. Mamta Rao was dead. He wondered what Rohit's plans were.

The assistant sheriff took it upon himself and ordered all flags at the police precincts to be flown half-mast too. The sheriff arrived and shared the information with the Red Cross where Mamta volunteered, the Salvation Army where Mamta ran a volunteer soup kitchen, and City Hall where Mamta and Rohit had donated a free clinic where they often volunteered for those who could not afford to pay for doctors.

Needless to say, the news affected the whole city of Cleveland in some fashion or other. Everyone felt the loss of a humanitarian. What had the militant group achieved? What is this irrational obsession to play with lives of fellow human beings?

Dr. Boss Man II arrived at the hospital. He was perplexed about all the flags in town being at half-mast. He was the only other doctor with the same specialization as Mamta, though his bedside manner was not anywhere close to that of Mamta's. He walked down to the nurse's station, with a question on his face.

Debbie saw his expression and filled him in on the course of events. "Last night the plane that Dr. Mamta was on crashed."

Dr. Boss Man II raised his hand with a clenched fist and pulled it down as he screamed, *"Yes!"*

Debbie had not expected that kind of reaction. All the nurses at the hospital despised this man for that kind of behavior. Of-course he had professional jealousy. Mamta had been offered the chairmanship of the wing and she had refused and let Dr. Boss Man II have it, so he could feel important. All the other nurses on shift that day actually wanted to see his reaction to the news. It didn't faze them, since they had expected it, though they had not anticipated the amount of jubilation shown. Whatever the jealousy, they had thought that some kind of compassion might be in him, but it was not there.

He lost the battle right there; he lost everyone's sympathy. People usually dig their own graves it is said. I guess those who do not actually enter the grave, live in this human hell.

Dr. Patel was the first to get the news of the Air India crash. He immediately knew that Mamta, who was on that flight, might have been lost. He called his cousin's brother, who worked at Toronto Airport and got confirmation that there were no survivors. It was in the early morning hours.

Dr. Patel took it upon himself to call all the Indian-immigrant families that lived in Cleveland. His wife Meeraben called around and all the ladies volunteered to make various dishes to take to Mamta's house.

It is customary not to let the bereaved family cook in their house for the first three days. As the morning light started to show up, there was a caravan of cars that approached Dr. Rao's home on the shores of Lake Erie. There were close to eight hundred cars of all different makes. Volunteers directed traffic. They allowed the people with food to get parking close to the house.

The ladies took over the house. They arranged for coffee and tea in the main foyer. They also brought with them disposable plates, spoons, and other paraphernalia. All this was accomplished without waking up Rohit, who was just getting a few winks. He did make out that there was something going on downstairs, but he did not care. His zest for life was gone. His mind had taken wing and flown away with the three souls that had visited him that night.

Dr. Chandru Patel was the first one to venture into Rohit's bedroom. As soon as his friend stepped into the room, Rohit saw him. "I have lost everything…Chandru…I lost everything."

Dr. Patel did not know how to console him. This is the plight of the first-generation immigrants. When they are in India growing up, they take things for granted. They are young in their teens and their parents and their families are young. They take for granted that their parents are going to live forever. They had always been shielded from the trauma of these kind of situations.

Suddenly faced with one, usually they are lost for words. They are lost as to how to express their innermost feelings. The only easy way out in these circumstances is just to let the emotional barriers be broken.

As adults, we always hide our emotions. We feel as grown-ups, we should not cry. Crying is what sissies do. It brings forth one's vulnerability. It makes one feel inferior. In this case, neither friend knew how to react, but both started to cry out loud.

All Dr. Patel muttered was, "I know…I know…how you feel."

Jose came in and brought Rohit his robe to wear over his nightclothes.

As he was handing over the robe, Rohit remembered Mamta. It had been her morning ritual to do that.

Jose remembered the promise he'd made to Mamta that he would take care of Rohit. He felt he had to make good on his promise.

Meeraben walked up the stairs with a cup of tea and entered the room. As soon as Rohit saw her, his emotions again took over, and he started to cry.

Women always have a way with words. "Mamta wouldn't want you to be discouraged."

Meera was the name of a great Indian saint, who sang folk songs in praise of the Lord. Meeraben continued, "One doesn't know the ways of God, why he does what he does. He doesn't let you in on his secret either. We have to wait and keep faith in him. Now take this tea, you need some nutrition."

It made absolutely no sense, but it sounded good. It comforted Rohit in its own way. The final result is what counts in the end.

Rohit took the tea, put on his robe, and started to come down. Meeraben felt she had accomplished what she'd gone up to do. "We have some food downstairs."

Meanwhile, Joanna and John drove to Birmingham, took a direct flight to Detroit, and showed up at Rohit's place as he was coming down the steps. The house was full of all the Indian families from the greater Cleveland area. In spite of that many people, there was pin-drop silence.

Rohit saw Joanna and John. He knew how much Joanne meant to his wife. He and John were good friends also. They were family. Two Indians, one British, and one American; what a bond they had created between them. As soon as he saw Joanna, the dam busted, and he came swiftly down the stairs and hugged her. Now there was no stopping him. He started to sob, cry, and express his inner feelings. Meeraben signed to all the visitors to clear the room to give them some privacy. Everyone there knew that John and Joanne were the Raos' family in Cleveland.

"You know I should have sent her to your anniversary, and this wouldn't have happened."

"You can't blame yourself for something that you had no control over."

"Joanna…you know Mamta wanted to postpone the journey by a day and I didn't listen."

Joanna just stayed silent

"I was doing what I thought was right and I was wrong. Joanna…Mamta always knew what was right and I should have listened to her. Now I have lost my whole family."

"Rohit listen, you have family still in India."

Rohit looked at her…

"Yes, you have the old couple. We have to take care of them."

"Yes, they cannot handle this news."

"We have booked tickets for you and me to go immediately."

"Yes, we have to take care of them."

Jose went upstairs, began gathering clothes, and started to pack bags.

Slowly, most of the people came up to Rohit and started to console him. One by one everyone in Cleveland, from the mayor, to the sheriff, a congressman, the hospital staff, and other prominent people arrived.

So did Dr. Boss Man II. All along the drive to the Raos, he was on the phone, discussing with his brother, Boss Man, the owner of the car dealership, about how he was going to take over Dr. Mamta Rao's lucrative practice.

At the house though, the minute he encountered Rohit, he explained how he would take care of Mamta's practice now that she was gone and how bad he felt that Seshi was also gone, otherwise she would have one day taken over the practice. He said he would do everything in his power to help out.

Rohit had no time for all this and asked Mamta's nurse to assist Dr. Boss Man II in taking over the office and all Mamta's cases.

Seshi's friend Mary had tears in her eyes, since she knew what her father and uncle were talking about in the car on the way. She ran into Seshi's room, which she was so familiar with, and threw up in the bathroom. Back in the bedroom, she sat on Sheshi's bed. Feeling that her friend was looking at her from the big portrait in the room, she couldn't help herself apologizing for her father and uncle, saying, "Seshi, I am sorry…I am sorry…I am sorry about them."

It looked as if she felt she was forgiven.

Chapter Fifteen

The river Godavari has its start in the Western Ghats in a place called Nasik, in India's state of Maharashtra. It flows from the northwestern side of the Deccan plateau down to the eastern side and enters the Bay of Bengal in an area called Konasema. Quite a few tributaries feed the river. It actually is the widest at Rajahmundry, a reasonable-sized town in the state of Andhra Pradesh. The river is approximately two miles wide at this place. It is here that the old British Raj decided to build a railway bridge.

As youngsters, Mamta and her friends would wait till the train from Madras reached the station at Kovvuru, where it started its tedious journey over the river across Godavari Bridge. The original bridge was flat without any steel structure. The train used to go past it at a very slow pace. The children aboard always used to get to the windows to throw copper coins into the river. "Three coins in the fountain, each one seeking happiness," was a song I heard in a movie. I used to wonder how many customs are universal but with different significance attached to them. The river in India has a very special meaning. Indian philosophy always talks about the ocean being the All Mighty. It has all the characteristics of being immense and omnipotent and omnipresent. It surrounds all the continents, and is a big contributor to the rainfall that is very much needed for agriculture. Rivers in the underdeveloped regions of the world are the source of primary irrigation. So they are revered and throwing coins into their beds shows gratitude. The other significance is that they are teachers to the students of nature. They are life sustaining and they teach that all thoughts should flow towards the mighty provider for the creatures on the land.

The river past Rajahmundry has close to seven sub-tributaries. These sub-tributaries form the delta regions. These regions at the mouth of the river, Godavari, are called Kona Seema. Every year at the time of the southwest monsoon, there is a very heavy rainfall in the western ghat region. That's the catchment area for the river Godavari and Rajahmundry was often flooded. Mamta's grandfather was a very smart man. He decided that he would build his house on a pedestal platform that was six feet high and made of concrete. On the top of this he built their ancestral home. During the floods, the water used to come close to four feet high and the family used to sometimes see cattle, fowl, dogs, and cats float away in the floodwaters. Most of them that could reach the house's safe platform usually tried to get on it. The worst of this kind were the cobras. As much as people revere them, they are literally petrified of cobras and so were Mamta and her family. The men used to stand guard to push them back into the water. Only one relative knew how to handle a snake; he could pick it up using a vantage point and throw it into the downside of the flow of water. Once the flood was over, every mango tree in the yard had so many of these critters housed on them it was forbidden for the children to approach them for at least three weeks. Some relatives raised few peacocks and peahens. The advantage was that these birds cleaned up the critters on the mango trees. Peacocks can eat cobras.

The delta regions were rich with very good alluvial soil deposits. This made it worthwhile for the agriculturists to live through the hardship of the floods, for their crops were abundant. The Kona Seema region was lush, green, and full of coconut groves. It was rather protected from the hustle and bustle and impact of urbanization.

Most of the supplies for these regions came from Rajahmundry. They loaded a launch, which is the local word for a barge. These launches left Rajahmundry in the morning around seven o'clock. They picked up the deliveries from the Calcutta mail train, which pulled in at six a.m.

In this region there were sparse electrical connections and most of the people used kerosene lamps. Most of the agriculture was rice fields and vegetable patches. The people all banded together and helped each other through thick and thin.

Mamta's grandfather and grandmother used to live in Rajahmundry, but they moved to the delta region for a more peaceful life. The delta region was close to forty miles wide and the was river spread out so that with their house on its platform, the impact of the floods was low.

These deltas had local officials called *Karanam*. Their job was to make sure that the surveys were kept up and any land transactions were recorded. Then there was the *munsab*, who took care of any utilities, such as roads and parks. In a place where there is no electricity, city water, or sewer, what else would be there to manage? But the munsab in Mamta's grandfather's village never gave up—he wanted his delta to have everything. To prove his point, he made sure that he was the only one who ran an electrical line and a phone line. Everyone in the village used his phone. He was also the only one who had a radio in his house. He was very much interested in technology. It was in the eighties that he heard that there was something coming called a digital revolution. So he held off on buying a TV till that digital system came.

The people in the area always helped each other out and were very close-knit. The whole town knew what was happening in each other's houses. It was a pristine area. Most of the older folk wanted to live in a place that still followed the old systems and culture. Towns usually had a temple, a main street, and a bridge on either side of the rivulets where vehicular traffic came. But it was closer if you used the launch to reach the community at Rajahmundry.

Mamta's grandfather was named Rammayya and her grandmother was Seethamma. Their house was on the outskirts of the town. It was a quaint place with an unpaved dirt road flanked with coconut palms. The road flowed through rice paddy fields and right now the rice stalks were in their prime and moved majestically as they waved in the wind. The sun was gentle. The road was sandier than soft dirt. The house had a compound wall and a gate in the front. On either side of the gate were two benches where people could sit and chat. Sculptures of squatting lions sat by the pillars on either side. An inside road led to the house and took a circular route, coming back after going under the portico. From the portico there were four steps to reach the elevated house's twelve-foot-wide verandah, which here we would call a wraparound porch.

Garu is a term of respect, and the people in the village called Mamta's grandfather, Rammayya garu. He always sat in an easy chair, which was long, rose in the back, and curled around for esthetics. It had straight legs in the front and curved legs in the back. Its armrests were four inches wide and extended all the way from the front to back. There were two leaves under the arm rests, which were pegged to the front legs and they could be rotated out to the front of the chair so the sitter could prop up their legs or use them to hold papers or write letters on.

Rammayya garu always sat there in the morning to read his paper. Seethamma garu, who was not expected to live much longer, was in the bedroom. Her pain was so immense she was completely drugged. She could hardly speak and was being taken care off by the grand old man. The people in the town helped them as much as they could. Rammayya garu always used to go to the munsab's house to call Cleveland. The munsab was a close family friend. He and his wife were like godparents to Mamta and had given *Kanyadanam* to Rohit during his and Mamta's wedding ceremony, which is similar to the Western practice of giving the bride away to the groom. Rohit was also very fond of the couple. The whole community was bubbling with joy in anticipation of Mamta's arrival. They had decorated their doorways with mango tree leaves, which are considered auspicious.

In the village, Sunday morning was moving along with high spirits and anticipation of at least few days of fun and frolic before the inevitable end of the grand old lady. Everyone felt that with her ripe old age, it was probably the right time for her to reach God's abode.

The water was plentiful that year because the northeast monsoon had dumped close to a hundred inches of rain in Chirapungi, the village that records the maximum rainfall in India year after year. Bobbarlanka had its share of the rainfall, which was reflected in the lush, green surroundings.

Rammayya garu made sure there was a pile of coconuts in the front yard, which had been specially selected by him and had their tops chopped off, ready to be punctured with a small hole to insert a straw to drink the coconut milk. Sunny and Seshi loved to drink coconut water. On the verandah was a basket full of ripe jamoons, a delicacy that Mamta liked. Alongside was a big basket with a lot of hay. In the hay were mangoes being seasoned to get ripe. There were two varieties of mangoes: banginipalli and rasam. Banginipalli was a large fruit with a lot of hard pulp that could be cut and served as a solid piece. The rasam was a variety that was very juicy and people usually punctured the tops and squeezed the juice into their mouths.

In the front of the house, one of the ladies was pouring water mixed with cow dung. The entryway into the house was greenish in color and looked as if it had been sprayed all around. The first smallpox vaccine had been developed when European scientists found that girls who were around cows affected with cowpox were immune from smallpox. Obviously this custom of spreading dung had been developed to offset potential smallpox. In the front yard they were decorating with muggu. These were intricate designs made with white lime powder.

It was nine a.m. when the munsab came in at the end of his morning walk. Rammayya garu was sitting in his easy chair with the Sunday edition of the *Indian Express,* which had been delivered that morning.

"*Namaskaram* Rammayya garu," said the munsab.

"*Namaskaram*" is the standard salutation in India; it's like, "Good morning. How do you do?" all put into one simple word. Word meanings get complex when the language is sophisticated. Latin and Sanskrit are two of the oldest languages and both have the capacity to express a multitude of feelings in simple words.

"*Namaskaram* Randi Munsab Garu," answered Rammayya garu.

PG explained to his listeners, "*Randi* means, 'Come in, please come in.' In the interest of keeping up the pace of the story, though, I will start delivering the interactions in English. In the movie there would be sub-titles of course."

Priya, Simrin, and Bob had just been listening, but then Bob reacted as if he'd suddenly awakened from a dream. "Do you mean to say you know that telo...goo..."

"It's Telugu. Phonetically, Tey Lou Gou...It is called the Italian of the East."

"What?"

"Joanne used say it should be the other way around. They should say Italian is the Telugu of the West."

"Do you speak Telugu?" Simrin asked, looking straight into PG's eyes.

"Yes, I do speak Telugu." There were tears in his eyes. He quickly wiped them off and shuffled his storyboards, trying to get back to the presentation.

"Did you visit Konaseema? Your description is beyond belief—your observation of the actual village and its concepts."

"Yes, we did spend a lot of moonlit nights…" He was lost for a minute in remembrance of the past but then he brought himself back. "Please, let's continue if I'm going to finish before Labor Day. I don't want to get blamed by Bob again."

"Sure, let's continue," said Priya. "May I have just a minute to hit the ladies room?"

Priya left the room and Simrin followed. Bob got up and headed off to the men's room, and PG was left alone. He broke down and started to weep. His emotions had taken the front seat. Men usually do not like to show their emotions. He got up and stood in front of the men's room door and as soon as Bob emerged, he dashed into the room, washed his face, and wiped off any traces of his emotional imbalance.

He came back into the room and started again on his narration:

"Munsab garu, please come and have a seat."

"Rammayya garu, it's a big day. All the children will be coming."

"Yes, they are your children too."

In a socially reinforced society, allowing neighbors to enforce discipline on other people's children is part of the social responsibility. For a very long time in India, the custom was followed and it still exists in the rural villages. This makes it difficult for unruly and unwanted elements to take hold in society. However, in recent years, urban sprawl has nullified this tradition.

"Munsab, you are being very gracious."

The two had formed a mutual admiration society.

"*Iyer*, please bring some coffee and *idlies* for our guest," said the old man.

Iyer is a cook, usually from the south, and an *idly* is a steam-cooked patty made with rice and lentil flour. A combination of carbs and protein all in one.

"Mamta and the kids must be in England now," said the munsab.

"No they must be still in the air. I believe that they will land in London about noon our time."

"Then it is only twelve hours to land in Bombay."

"It's funny that it takes less time to cross oceans than it does to come from Bombay to Bobbarlanka."

They laughed as Iyer appeared with two plates of *idlies* and cups of coffee.

"Is the boy I arranged for bringing your paper on time?"

"Yes he is here within few minutes of the launch whistle."

"That's good. It seems I cannot get you to put electricity in your home. Neither can I get you to put in a telephone."

"You know that I grew up with kerosene lamps, a slate for a book. and a *raachippa*[7] for chalk."

"That does not mean that you cannot grow with industrialization."

"There' a price to pay for everything in this world."

"What do you mean?"

"God in his creation gave man the power of choice."

"He gave it to animals also."

"No, he gave them a particular process. Suppose you put a human baby and a calf in a protected environment, without any interaction with the outside world."

"Without food?" asked the munsab, eating his *idly*.

"Give them food—it is essential. The calf will grow up just like any other cow and will mature and do everything as it should do."

"And?"

"The human baby will be lost because its development is based on its interaction with other people in the beginning and its choices as it grows older."

"I guess that's the reason we have engineers and doctors."

"I guess. Well tomorrow early morning, the kids will be here."

"I cannot wait to hear Sunny and Seshi speak Telugu with that American accent."

"Neither can I."

"Well, I have to go now. I have a meeting with the karanam garu. We are going to decide if we should approach the government to give us money to electrify the delta."

"Why?" said Rammayya with a disgusted expression.

"So we can have a permanent movie theatre."

That sealed it. Rammayya garu did not want to hear another word. "Please go and do your meetings. I really hope that by the time you do all the damage I will be long gone."

"Rammayya garu, look at it this way. All our kids who come back from America, especially our grandkids, would want to have a TV to watch that game called football where they play with their hands."

---

[7] *Raachippa* is a lime-derived utensil, which when broken was used as chalk.

"Yes, those Cleveland Browns."

"See, you understand."

"I guess when it comes to grandkids, everything goes."

"So do I have your support to get electricity?"

"Yes. You have my support."

"Are you coming to the meeting?"

"No. I have to get organized for their arrival. They will be here tomorrow morning at nine."

"Do I have your proxy then?"

"Yes. You can have my proxy."

"I will see you later—the meeting is at eleven."

In this village of twenty-five households, every household had a vote in village affairs. Many trusted Rammayya garu. He had a following of at least fifteen families. That's why the munsab always wanted to get his blessing on major agenda items before putting them up for votes.

The sun started to blast as the 10:30 mark arrived. People from the neighboring village, who were working in the fields, started to cover their heads with white cloths. The breeze from the vast expanse of water all around was moist and cool. There seemed to be a tug-of-war between the hot sun and the cool breeze.

The meeting was a landmark one. Even though many wanted to vote for electricity, they had not been willing to go against Rammayya garu. They all felt he had good reasons when he opposed an issue and that it was for the common good and not for political reasons.

The village meetings were held under a banyan tree in front of the munsab's house. He had ordered a gross of Pepsi Cola bottles with straws. They were put in ice that had been brought from Rajahmundry. This was a treat for the participants. Of course, it could also be considered a bribe to gain votes.

The meeting was delayed by thirty minutes because the quorum was not met. India is a very democratic country despite its scandals about buying votes.

By 11.45 a.m., all the townspeople had gathered around the tree. The meeting was called to order.

"You cannot start the meeting without Rammayya garu," one of the older gentleman shouted.

"Yes, yes," some in the crowd agreed.

"I have been to his house this morning and he is busy. As all of you already know, Mamta and her kids are coming tomorrow morning."

"Yeah, yeah."

"He has given me the proxy to vote on issues on his behalf."

"Did he agree for electrifying?" an eager beaver asked.

The munsab waited a minute and people started to get anxious.

"He...He...supports the electricity project."

Everyone started to clap and cheer. The sound reached Rammayya's ears and he immediately knew that the Electricity Project had gotten the nod from the village elders.

Just then, the munsab's son bolted out of the house saying, "Nanna garu, come inside for a minute. It's urgent."

The way he came out, every one there knew that something was wrong. The munsab ran inside, and the whole group outside came closer to the house. The munsab's son increased the volume on the radio so everyone could hear the broadcast. They all listened, trying to understand what was going on.

"Unconfirmed reports are suggesting that there are no survivors from the crash of the Air India plane *Emperor Kanishka*. Again, recapping the breaking news...It is reported on the wire that an Air India plane has crashed into the northern Irish Sea. The aircraft, the *Emperor Kanishka* was en-route to London from Montreal. Unconfirmed reports are suggesting that all the passengers are dead aboard the Air India plane, *Emperor Kanishka*. We will keep you informed as we receive more details...Now back to the scheduled program: listener's requests."

There was absolute silence. Some gathered there did not even know what it meant. There was a somber mood in the gathering. Suddenly, breaking the silence, Munsab's wife started to cry, and she said to her husband, "Does that mean our daughter Mamta is no more?"

The significance hit everyone then. There was a collective sigh.

"Someone has to tell Rammayya garu," one blurted out.

"Hold your horses," said Munsab in a stern voice. "Let's get back to the meeting and figure out what to do."

Everyone started to wipe their tears. Each had his or her own way to cope with the news. Some expressed their thoughts.

"How do we know that they were on that flight?" said Shetty. He was the storekeeper who always wanted to know if the merchandise was on the train or not.

"The old lady is on her last days, that's why they were coming—we better be sure before we tell them anything."

"Let's not create a new problem for Rammayya and Seethamma."

"Especially when we do not know for sure."

"Isn't it ironic that their lives were taken before Seethamma's?"

"You don't know that," protested a good friend of Seethamma's.

"This is un-natural. This is not the way the rules were written."

"Yes, the old should precede the young when it comes to death."

"Why does God always punish the good people in the world?"

"He must be testing them, I guess."

"We shouldn't keep it a secret," said Harischandra. Harischandra was one who always spoke the truth.

Munsab was getting irritated, not because everyone was expressing opinions, but because he did not have a proper course of action.

His son seemed to be making it a habit to bolt out of the house. This time he had a message for his dad. "Aunty Joanne is on the phone for you, Dad."

Everyone in the crowd knew Joanne, who had often visited with Mamta. Their hopes rose.

"If Joanne has called, it means that they are OK."

"Yes, those two are always together."

The crowd's spirits had gotten a boost and they hoped that the news on the radio was just a false alarm. Munsab ran into the house to answer the phone call. The whole group no longer cared about appearances. They followed him in to overhear the conversation.

"This is Uncle Munsab here."

"Hi Uncle. I have some bad news."

"Don't tell me it is about…" He put it on speakerphone so everyone could hear it.

"Uncle listen. I'm in England. I just heard the news of the crash. We don't know for sure about survivors. I know Rohit well enough to know he must be completely off-kilter."

"Please take care of him…he is a nice boy," Munsab said.

"Uncle, I am leaving right now for Cleveland and will be there with him. Then we both will come to India to be with the grandpa and ma. This is what you have to do."

This was the welcome direction everyone had been waiting far.

"Joanne, we will follow your instructions to the tee."

"Uncle, I am concerned about Grandpa and Ma. They will not be able to take the news."

"We agree," the whole group said.

"Am I on speaker phone?"

"Yes you are…Thalli…we were having a council meeting."

"Good, that means everyone is there…Don't let anyone talk about this till we both come. Just tell Grandpa that there was change of plans and that we're all going to be there day after tomorrow."

"Yes, we will do that," said Munsab.

"Uncle, Grandpa has not bought a radio as yet, right?"

"No, he didn't. He usually comes here to listen to the nine p.m. news."

"Good, make sure he misses the news tonight."

"How will you get here by the day after tomorrow?" Munsab thought it was impossible.

"Uncle, I have reservations on the Concorde to Paris and then a connection to Madras and to Bezawada. From there we will take a car. OK? Make sure he doesn't get the news till we get there. We will see you in couple of days. I have to go, my flight is being called." The phone was disconnected.

There was a sigh from everyone. Everyone felt a little calmer since it was established that the bad-news bearers would be Rohit and Joanne.

Munsab was trying to think up a plan to keep Rammayya from listening to the news that night.

As if God sent, a messenger arrived from Rammayya's house. "My master wanted me to tell you that he will not be coming this evening to hear the news."

The whole group was relieved, including Munsab, and they were careful not to let out the terrible secret they were holding.

Munsab wanted to make sure that Rammayya would not change his mind, so he sent him a message back. "Tell him that I was going to send him a message. This evening I have a meeting in Rajahmundry, and won't be coming back till late at night. My whole family is going with me to see a movie."

The messenger departed.

Munsab turned to the group. "Listen carefully everyone, we all have to be very diligent. We cannot have a slip. So let's ask one of our local village guards to intercept any one going to Rammayya's house this evening."

"Yes, we should do that," everyone agreed.

"Pollyanna, you be there discreetly, guarding who goes to their house and who comes out. Tomorrow, in the morning, I will go there to inform Rammayya of the change in plans."

Everyone agreed and the plans were set. The village mourned the loss of Mamta and the kids. They felt bad for Rohit. They did not know what the daybreak would bring, and they were worried about how the old lady was going to take the news.

By dark all the people in the village were sitting on the front verandahs and talking about the Rammayya family.

In the temple prayers were lifted, requesting that it not be true.

The people reminisced about the good old days when the kids were young and played in the streets of the village. Some older folk talked about Mamta's parents and their stories. All in all, the mood was somber. Pollyanna stood vigil till late night and as it turned midnight, he decided that he would head home to sleep.

All the lights in the village were shut off, with the exception of Munsab's house where there was an electric lamppost in the front yard that was kept lit all night. There was an eerie feeling in everyone. Nobody slept; everyone tossed around, pre-occupied with thoughts on future events.

The Calcutta mail train was on the other bank of the river, Godavari. It plugged slowly along the bridge and the children on the train were getting ready to throw copper coins into the river. The Canadian engine gave out a loud whistle and the whole area around heard it. The baggage car clerk was busy, getting ready to disperse his goods in Rajahmundry.

He had prioritized his deliveries. The first to be unloaded were the newspapers: *The Hindu*, *The Indian Express*, *The Patrika*. They all had the details on the crash. The vendors usually picked-up the papers from the train and distributed them.

The train puffed into Rajahmundry Station. The papers were unloaded and Shetty's representative took a bundle to the launch.

Soon, the launch made it to Bobbarlanka where three young boys were waiting to make deliveries. The oldest one picked-up the bundle and took two *Indian Express* papers and gave them to the other two boys. They took to their bikes, rode together to the munsab's house, delivered one paper, and were on their way.

Munsab had not had a good night's sleep and was lethargic in getting up. He washed his face, took his cup of coffee, and opened the paper. The front-page news was about the crash and it said to look to page two for the names of the passengers that were on the plane.

He dropped his expensive china coffee cup and saucer and opened to the second page. There were the names of Mamta, Seshi, and Sunny of Cleveland, USA. In a heartbeat, Munsab recalled that he had arranged for the papers to be delivered first to himself and then to Rammayya garu.

For a moment, he did not know what to do, but then he got up and ran toward the Rammayya house to stop delivery of the paper. Shetty realized the situation at the same time, and started to run in the same direction. The priest in the temple saw both of them and followed. Soon, everyone in the village who saw them followed at a run. They all arrived at the house at the same time.

They entered the house and found Rammayya relaxing on his easy chair with the *Indian Express* spread on his face. Munsab found his courage and said out loud, "Rammayya garu. Rammayya garu."

There was neither reply nor any movement. From farther inside the house, the bedridden Seethamma shouted, "I have been calling him for half an hour. He doesn't answer."

Munsab did not know what to do. He approached the easy chair. "Rammayya garu…Rammayya garu." He removed the *Indian Express*.

Rammayya's face was still wet with tears. He had learned his dear grand-daughter Mamta was no more.

Munsab wept to see his friend's face with the eyes still open. The old man had a calm countenance. He was dead.

Alas, now it was the old lady's turn.

God has his own ways that we cannot comprehend.

There was silence in the room.

At the offices of RLS Productions, everyone was teary eyed. Priya suggested they break for the day.

They needed a break. So they dispersed to reconvene early the next morning.

Man proposes and God disposes…

The million-dollar question is…

Whose God?

Chapter Sixteen

Next morning, the foursome was punctual and the threesome was ready to hear what would transpire at Bobbarlanka. PG started his narration again.

Speechless, Munsab stood in front of Rammayya. The village elders joined him up on the elevated platform while the rest of the crowd stood and watched.

"Munsab garu, what is happening there?" shouted Seethamma from her bed where she'd been confined for the past six months, unable to get up and Munsab nor anyone there had any idea as to how to inform her of this turn of events.

"Munsab, your silence is bothering me. What's happening?"

Seethamma had dropped the garu. Usually it only happens when one is very annoyed with the situation or when one wants to take charge. Munsab didn't know which was the reason in this case. He himself was lost for words. He did not know what course of action he should take. He turned around and saw half of the town standing there, not knowing what to do next. In the crowd was a small, six-year-old girl. She looked at all the people and their tear-filled faces. A child usually doesn't understand the frailties of human behavior.

Seethamma called out again. "Munsab! Please tell me what's happening. My husband never ignores me; he always acknowledges me. Is he OK? The last I heard him was when he said aloud, 'Mamta, my dear.' Please fill me in what's happening—you know my disability."

Munsab did not know what to do. He was weeping but he could not cry out loud lest she figure out that there was something wrong out there. What were they all thinking? That they were going to keep everything from her? The news of the calamity? The old man's dead body? This was a no-win situation. Everyone was worried that the old lady would not be able to handle the news and that she would collapse, or even follow suit with her husband. No one was ready to be the reason for that possibility.

"*Munsab!!*" shouted Seethamma. I guess her patience was wearing thin. The little girl didn't know what all the fuss was about. For her, death was not a reality yet. She was young and did not even know what death meant. Her mother had told her recently that death meant someone going to a long sleep because they were too tired.

The child decided to take things into her own hands. Without anyone noticing, she slowly went inside and got to the room where Seethamma was bedridden. As she came in, Seethamma saw her walking towards her. She knew she could extract from this child what was happening out there. Munsab and the group of elders were still formulating the strategic direction they should take.

The girl's name was Nijman. Ironically, it meant truth. She was the granddaughter of the priest in the temple. When she'd seen her grandfather running, she followed him to see what was happening. It had been the night before when they were talking about Aunty Mamta that she had pestered her mom to explain what death was and was given the meaning. This was her recently acquired knowledge.

"Nijam, *thalli*, come here and tell me what's happening."

"Grandma…Grandma…you know…you know…" Nijam slowly tried to tell the old woman what was happening. Her fluency in the language was not at its best as yet. But she did express herself very well.

"My dearest Nijam, you are my friend aren't you? Tell me."

"Grandma…yesterday…"

"Yesterday what happened?"

"Yesterday everyone was crying."

Seethamma was sure it had something to do with Mamta. "Don't be afraid, tell me everything. You know I cannot even get up from here." Seethamma was trying to introduce some logic into the equation.

"Mamta…Aunty Mamta…Aunty went to a long sleep."

"Mamta went to a long sleep? What about Sunny and Seshi?"

"They all went to a long sleep with the plane."

Seethamma figured out what that meant. Now she had to find out what was going on outside. She had tears in her eyes. "Tatagaru …what is he doing?"

"Tata…garu also went to a long sleep reading the paper."

Seethamma took Nijam, hugged her, and said, "True to your name, you tell the truth, don't you?"

"That's why they named me Nijam."

"Nijam *thalli*. You know, when people go to a long sleep, it is we who are awake who have to take care of people."

"Grandma, I will take care of you."

"We both have to take care of Uncle Rohit."

"I will help you, Grandma."

"Sure, get me that saree from there and ask Uncle Munsab to wait there for me."

"I will."

"Nijam, my dear Nijam."

Nijam went and fetched the saree and gave it to Seethamma. Then she slowly walked onto the verandah. Munsab, the priest, and the rest of the company were still wondering what to do. They were all lost. Suddenly, there was this little girl trying to get Munsab's attention, by yanking on his pants.

He knelt down. "Nijam what is it?"

"I told Grandma everything."

"What did you tell?"

"That Tata garu went to a long sleep."

"What?" That's all he could say. He was surprised how simple the solution was. *Tata went to a long sleep.*

"Grandma wants you to wait here for her."

This came as a further surprise.

"I am going to help Grandma to take care of Uncle Rohit."

That meant that Seethamma had also figured out about Mamta. The whole group was amazed at how things have a way of getting resolved. They still were not sure how to go about the next few days. Everyone had their own interpretation of the events to follow. The group knew that Rohit was on his way and that he still didn't know about the latest turn of events.

A big surprise was in store for them. Suddenly, they saw some movement from inside the house. There was the curtain being removed by someone, but slowly, with a shaking hand. A foot crossed the main threshold and slowly the struggling Seethamma walked out and addressed her gardener, who was in the crowd. "Anjani, please make me a walking stick. I think I need it now."

The whole crowd was stunned. For the past six months she had been bedridden with cancer. She could not even move from one side of the bed to the other. But for the help of Rammayya, she was an invalid. It had been pronounced that she had only six months to live. For all practical purposes, she was considered dead by the whole village. Now she had walked out under her own steam. Her voice was very firm and authoritative. It looked like she was on a mission.

She struggled to walk to the easy chair where Rammayya was. The newspaper was on the floor. She looked at Nijam with an implied *please help me* look. Nijam came running, held her hand, helped her to the spot, and picked up the paper and gave it to her. Everyone else there was still looking at this old lady and wondering how she'd gotten up and was walking around.

Humans have this specific problem associated with convictions. First of all, convictions are not necessarily all good nor right. People with dogmatic convictions should be convicted. Conviction rises out of a lot of layers of ignorance. It is essential that one should first attempt to remove the veils of ignorance before one becomes dogmatic with his or her conviction. Conviction blinds people so they can even forget what kind of circumstances they are really in. Other than the respect they had for this old couple, there was nothing holding back some of the ladies in the group. They had always respected Rammayya and Seethamma for their knowledge and devotion to God, along with their daily prayer routine. But conviction feeds and causes the ultra-egos of humans to flourish. All the right combinations were there and slowly there were whispers and ladies biting each other's ears off with their convictions.

Focus was diverted from the main issue and the discussion among the ladies was about who among them was going to reinforce the age-old dogmatic convictions. The widow, first of all, should wear white clothes and no jewelry. She should stay inside and mourn and not wear *kumkum*.[8]

---

[8] A colored powder used for social and religious markings.

Contrary to this, Seethamma had come out wearing a blood-red saree, and she was decked out in her normal jewelry with a large red dot of *kumkum* on her forehead. This went against the convictions of some of the ladies. There were some who defended Seethamma by saying she was above all convictions because she was a *Jnani* or learned. Seethamma was well aware of the people who surrounded her, and she was especially aware of their hang-ups. She also knew who out of the whole bunch would be very active in this respect. As she was looking at the newspaper, reviewing the names of the casualties, she simultaneously started calling out the trouble mongers. "Mandara, Suryakala, Anasuya, Swarna, please come here."

The whole group immediately understood what was happening. Some of the people were angry that these ladies were talking about frivolous things and were not in tune with the situation.

The ladies realized that Seethamma had picked up on their whispers. They were actually stunned as how to she could hear them. They had been standing at least fifty feet away, at the back of the crowd.

The ladies slowly climbed up to the verandah and meekly stood apart from Seethamma, but she summoned them closer. She was on one side of the easy chair and they stood on the other side with the relevant issue between them.

"*Thallulaara*[9]... see him, he is sleeping. Nijam told me that death is going to a long sleep. Any relationship in this world is based on one's mental association with the other. It is one's fixation in the mind that matters. If your husband went on a long trip, would you forget him completely? As long as your mental faculty can remember him, he is still very much alive. He is not dead until he is completely forgotten by everyone. Under those circumstances do you think these dogmatic convictions should be followed?"

The group of ladies shook their heads, kind of agreeing with her philosophy.

"That's why I am wearing a blood-red saree. This signifies that from now on I have to be on the path of self-realization and godly pursuit. This is Lalithamma's color."

The four ladies were speechless.

Seethamma dismissed the ladies and said, "Please, Munsab garu...let us figure out what we need to do from now onward. Is Sastry here?"

"I sent word for him."

---

9 An affectionate salutation in Telugu

As he was saying that, Sastry came running and stood in front of them.

"Sastry garu, please tell me what we should do," said Seethamma.

"Amma, first we should put a jute mat on the floor and move him on to it. We should immediately light a small oil lamp and place it beside him near his head."

"Anjani, where are you?" called Seethamma.

"Amma, I just completed your walking stick."

So saying, Anjani came up and gave her the walking stick. As if he'd known what was going to be asked next, he also had a jute mat with him.

As if to make right the wrong they had done, the four ladies immediately cleared a spot, sprinkled it with water, and wrote the word Om on it with some chalk powder. Then one of them brought an oil lamp to put there. Everyone now was focused on the main issue.

"Amma, we should arrange for the cremation of the mortal remains; it should be done before sunset."

"First let us talk of something more important. Do we have to call Rohit?" She questioned the munsab, as she knew he would be the one who would receive any information from the United States.

"I had a call from Joanne about the plane." He could not get himself to speak about Mamta's and the kids' demise.

"What should we do about the kids?" asked Sastry, who unfortunately did not know about the plane crash. "Mamta and Rohit can perform the last rites together."

Seethamma understood the predicament. No one there wanted to acknowledge the passing away of the kids in the plane crash. She turned to Sastry and said, "Mamta, Seshi, and Sunny are no longer with us except for fond memories, just like him." For the first time she had tears in her eyes. They trickled down her cheeks and she didn't even care to wipe them. "Their mortal remains might not be available, so what are our options?"

Sastry was also now in a quandary as what to do. He had never faced a situation like this before, but he came up with a brilliant idea. "We will make a funeral pyre for each of them and perform the rituals as usual. We have to hurry because it has to be done before sunset."

Seethamma was getting irritated at being told it had to be completed before sunset. "We have to wait for Rohit to come. It may take a couple of days."

"Amma, we cannot do because the body will deteriorate. We will be sorry that we did it. There is no hospital close by either, to keep it in cold storage. The best we can do is we can schedule it for tomorrow. The body should be out of the house within a day, it is said."

"I know Rohit will be here. We have to wait for him."

"If he makes it by tomorrow morning, otherwise we have to proceed as planned."

"Rohit will be here. Make arrangements for the four funeral pyres: one for him and three others for his three favorite people." Tears rolled down her eyes again but her composure was to be commended.

The arrangements were made for the funerals. The news had by now reached the whole delta area and there were visitors coming from far and near to pay respects to the grand old man and comfort the grand old lady. The night set in but there were people in the house throughout the night. The oil lamp was watched and refueled time to time. Eventually, the early morning approached. The sun reluctantly rose in the eastern sky. Sastry pronounced that the body should move out of the house by 8:30. The time was ticking but the old lady insisted that they should wait for Rohit. Everyone in the village was there. The 8.15 a.m. whistle of the launch was heard.

"Rohit is on that launch…let us wait till he gets home," said Seethamma.

There were two cyclists spotted about two miles from the house.

"They are coming Grandma…on cycles," said Nijam and comforted her.

The two cyclists came close and leaving the cycles on the road ran into the house. It was Joanne who ran in first and she froze in front of the body and was speechless for a moment. As soon as she understood what was in front of her, she began to cry. "Rohit, we are too late…God damn it…we are too late…We are just too late…Why? Why? What did we do?"

Rohit came running in and seeing the body just stood there with tears running down his cheeks. He looked around to see where Seethamma was and spotted her sitting in a chair. She arose and started to walk towards him.

Joanne was still fixed on Rammayya's body. He had treated her as he did Mamta. There was a bond between them.

Rohit started to walk to the grand old lady. They both had been very composed till then. He came very close to her and with tears flowing down, said in a quivering voice, "Mamta left me and now Tata left me…I am alone."

In an authoritative voice, Seethamma said, "I am there for you…I am there for you…I will take care of you…don't you worry."

They hugged and for the first time both of them started to cry out loud… and looking at Joanne, Seethamma, said, "Tata left us…yes Tata left us… so did Mamta…now we have to take care of Rohit…we have to take care of Rohit."

"Yes Grandma…I know…Mamta took a promise from me." So saying, Joanne joined in the hug. The three of them started to cry and hug each other.

The time approached. Sastry asked Rohit to take the water that was there and to drench himself and with his wet clothes, lead the procession to the cremation ground. There Rohit saw the four pyres. Joanne broke down again and started to cry out loud and so did he. He then was asked to do the ritualistic carrying of water around the pyres.

It was now time for him to light the pyres. He started with the oldest's pyre, Rammayya's, followed by Sunny's. Next to it was Mamta's and the last one was for Seshi.

As he lit the fire he was overcome with sorrow. She was his darling daughter. She had done everything he had asked her to do and she was no more. The realization came. He saw Joanne and weeping said "Seshi also left me… Sunny left me."

All that was left for them was to mourn the departed.

There was a haunting question, which was asked again and again.

What did Rammayya, Mamta, Seshi, and Sunny have to do with whatever that terrorist group wanted? They were neither connected nor implicated. They were unfortunate victims of the indiscriminate behavior of people with convictions, who should have been convicted.

Convictions do not stand up to logical interpretation.

The three listeners at RLS Productions did not utter a word. They were just listening. I guess every one needed a break. Not saying a word, each one found their own place of silence.

Often, silence is golden.

Chapter Seventeen

It was unusual that the foursome met at the Starbucks by chance rather than by design. Priya and Bob had already completed their morning meeting. They both felt they had something they could produce well. Bob felt that PG had to be handled with kid gloves and he put the responsibility on Priya and Simrin. That was when they spotted Simrin and PG walking towards the Starbucks. Priya commented that Simrin and PG had some chemistry between them and she was going to take advantage by getting Simrin to deal with him. Bob was concerned that the presentation would drag right into Labor Day and their plans to close the business for a ten-day vacation might have to get cancelled. Priya assured him that PG knew of that complication and that he would complete before the month ended.

"Good morning, PG," Bob greeted him.

"Good morning, sir. Shall we begin early today? We have only three days to complete the presentation."

"Please don't rush, you're doing fine." This was the first time Bob had put in an effort to be nice.

"Mr. Stevenson, I have to get this on celluloid—that's my dream."

"We will get it on celluloid after we finalize…"

"I don't need any money. It doesn't have any value. Hasn't my story conveyed that message already? Money is a temporary intoxication that does not follow you where you are ultimately going."

"You are absolutely right."

"Help me get it out on celluloid with proper direction and the pathos it provides. Let my audiences know the true meaning of life and death. Let the indiscriminate individuals understand that the people they punish don't deserve it…they don't deserve it."

"Let's get going," Bob said, feeling uncomfortable again.

The foursome walked down the street without a word spoken. Together they climbed the front steps of the office building, entered the front lobby, and turned towards the elevators. Bob took to the stairs as usual.

"Does he always do this?." PG enquired as they entered the office.

"Yes, he is a health nut," Priya said.

"He takes care of himself," Simrin added, putting her coat on the hanger in the closet.

Priya went to her office and PG parked himself on the sofa in the lobby. "How long does it take for him to climb?" he asked.

"Twenty-five minutes and he comes up drenched."

"Hum. May I make some coffee?"

"Please do."

Bob soon entered, sweating, and headed off to his office to shower saying, "It shouldn't take but a minute."

Simrin went into the conference room and closed the blinds. Priya walked out of her office, poured a cup of coffee, and headed into the conference room. PG followed her and started to put up a storyboard with a front view of the Rao residence. There was a caption at the bottom. "Three Years Later."

Bob walked in and so did Simrin. Suddenly Bob excused himself saying, "PG, give me just few minutes…I have to call my wife and kids."

"Please go ahead, we will wait."

Simrin looked at Priya as if this was a new thing and a departure from his normal behavior. Priya acknowledged Simrin with an expression that it was. Their facial expressions could have filled a million pages.

PG had an expression on his face that suggested he was pleased that his aim for the presentation had been fulfilled. He was getting the anticipated response. If he could get the same response from audiences, it would make his day. If he could get this message to the indiscriminate terrorists, it would be just fine.

Bob came back with glee on his face from having talked to his wife.

PG started the narration again.

Three years had passed since the Air India crash. It was found that there had been a bomb planted on the aircraft by some militant group who wanted their own state. So they killed a planeload of passengers, who had no clue as to what hit them. In the process they'd affected so many innocent people. There has got to be a better way to resolve conflicts.

After the tragedies that hit the Rao family, the only thing Rohit could do was to bring the grand old lady to Cleveland. After getting the fortified food in the United States, she gained strength and slowly started to beat the cancer. It took the route of remission.

Look at the irony of life.

Rao was so depressed and with the old lady in the house, requested that John and Joanne move in next door and be with him and help him. They bought the mansion next door and moved in. Typing furiously on his typewriter, John recorded all the events that had transpired in their lives. He made it till the plane crash and then hit writer's block. The clanking of the typewriter stopped. He did not know where to go from there.

Joanne was sleeping on her king size mattress with satin sheets. She wore a very sexy negligee. Her face was pure and very calm. I guess when you have pure thoughts and a sweet disposition it's reflected in how your skin forms itself. A wrinkled face is always a giveaway of the kind of life one leads.

Joanne had always led a chaste life. She prioritized her life based on her conscience. Anything she felt was not in good spirit she avoided. John was a companion who had been made in Heaven for her. It looks as though Cupid always makes the best choice, taking into consideration the chemistry between people. At least in the case of John and Joanne, it was a perfect match.

Joanne was his companion, friend, mentor, and guiding light. John was a puritan with utopian ideas. For him, the whole world was a good place. People often took advantage of him in very many ways. He was a beloved target of scam artists. Joanne was his saving grace.

She put her arm on the side of the bed where John slept, found it empty and instinctively felt the bed. It was cold, suggesting that he had not been there for a while. Usually she heard his typewriter clanking. There were no sounds in the room. She sat up in the bed and looked for him. She knew he would not have left the room. So she started to look around to find where he was. If he saw her up, he would always say, "Hi my angel, you are up."

She did not hear that sweet voice either. She scanned the room and then spotted him on the terrace adjoining the bedroom. She at once knew something was bothering him, so she got up and put on a matching robe. She slowly started to walk to the open terrace. The moon was shining from the south, filling the area with a blue tint and the softness that is always associated with moonlight.

There was a time when the moon was a prerequisite for every romantic situation. Many a song has been written with the moon as an intruder into love affairs. The moon had seen many romances, many infatuations, many curiosity seekers, and many experimenters in cars, in gardens, under trees, on terraces, and in very many different permutations and combinations. Every Broadway show had to have a song with the moon involved.

John was sitting on a chair close to the railing. The moon cast a shadow of the roofline just behind him. He was looking out onto Lake Erie, which was blanketed with the moonlight. Joanne was clad in white silk. She looked like an angel. She parted the drapes of the double door, which were gently moving and fluttering in the breeze coming off the lake. It was the third anniversary of the crash.

Joanne slowly stepped behind John without making any noise. She did not want to disturb him if he was asleep. Her shadow was cast on him. He knew she was behind him.

"Hi my angel, you are up."

"I missed you."

"I didn't want to disturb your peaceful sleep."

"You should have. Do you know how long it has been since we both sat like this on a moonlit night?"

"Three years."

"Don't tell me you've been counting."

"No."

"Three years?"

"Yes, today is the third year."

"Already three years."

They saw a white glow in the northern sky. It gave them the feeling that it was looking at them. Neither knew what to make of it. When they looked to their left they saw Rohit out on his terrace staring at the light. And there was Jose, standing at the steps leading to the lake looking at the light.

"Do you remember last year there was a news item on the TV?" said John.

"Which one?"

"They talked about this glow that was spotted in the northern sky. It kind of shone towards Cleveland."

"Yes."

"It's the same light again."

"How do you know?" she asked.

"It was on this exact day last year at this exact hour."

"What exact hour?"

"One twenty."

Joanne realized that when she'd gotten up it had been 1:18.

"This is the exact time the plane crashed."

Joanne had goosebumps all over. She was not at all comfortable. But the thought of her dear friend Mamta suddenly calmed her beyond belief. She did not know what to make of the whole thing.

"Are you saying what I'm thinking?"

Why do we always try to hide supernatural issues?

"Yes, I think it is Mamta's soul." John always had an extra-sensory perception and could make out many supernatural happenings. "See, it will disappear in a moment."

Just as he predicted, it started to fade. Suddenly it grew bright again, and as if it had found something it loved very much, it started to streak down onto the terrace where Joanne was standing. Then, with a swoosh, it climbed back up to the sky, diminished, and vanished.

"See, I told you it was Mamta. She was saying hi to you."

Joanne was not scared but felt a kind of warmth from the bright light and a feeling of affection. John got up from his chair and hugged her. They hugged for few minutes.

"Is something bothering you?" Joanne asked.

"No."

"Don't hide it. Something is really bothering you."

"Writer's block."

"Where are you?"

"Just finished the crash."

"Then?"

"Don't know where to go from there."

"Write about the three years thereafter."

"What do you mean?"

"Write about Seethamma and her recovery."

"That's a good idea."

"Write about the human psyche."

"What?"

"Humans always need to have someone or something that occupies the brain. When the brain is active and fertile, it makes the rest of the body perform in order to fulfill the wants of the brain."

"Keep going."

"Ordinary people, they all need this kind of stimulation. Only those sages in ancient India conquered the wanting of wants and still managed to live long lives."

"No. They had one overwhelming want, which was to understand the true nature of God."

"Till they found the truth they lived."

"But there is always a catch to this."

"What?"

"God doesn't want you to know his real self. He wants it to be a secret as long as the universe exists. It's the universal secret."

"What do you mean?"

"When one of the sages found out the truth, he immediately had nothing to live for, as his quest was complete. He didn't want anything else other than to reach the Almighty. So his brain voluntarily let him leave this bodily existence and migrate into the universal existence. We always feel that we need a huge mass of fuel to speed up to warp speeds. That is not true."

"Then what?"

"The weight and mass of the soul is so small and insignificant it can accelerate at the speed of light and beyond—something like the accelerator used to break atoms in Chicago."

"That's why you feel that the light we saw was Mamta."

"Precisely."

Joanne thought for a beat. "Then the reason Seethamma is in remission is a very simple reason."

"You figured it out."

"Yes, when she found that Rohit was all alone and had no one else to take care of him, she took it upon herself to take care of him."

"That's why as soon as she came here she started the route to rehabilitation and is now walking on her own and taking care of the house…of course with a lot of assistance from my angel."

"Now you've got an idea to work on to end the novel in the perfect way. Write about all this."

"Thank you, Joanne. I don't know what I would do without you."

"Come, let's go to bed. We have a busy schedule tomorrow."

They walked hand in hand to the bed and got under the sheets.

Isn't Cupid wonderful? They call him *Manmadha* in Sanskrit.

Man means heart. Madhu means nectar, wine, honey, and those that can make you intoxicated. Manmadha is the one who intoxicates one's heart.

I guess it is called love.

Chapter Eighteen

John, as usual, got out of bed and went to the corner where his typewriter was. He was adamant that he would use his old Underwood from the good old country. Some con artist had sold him the antique, saying that it was the typewriter on which PG Wodehouse wrote all his novels. Seshi had presented him with an Apple Macintosh Computer. It adorned the table as if it were an antique, while his reliable Underwood did all the work. The chitter and the chatter from the typing, the nice bell suggesting the end of the line, and the swish sound of manually moving the paper carriage to start the next line were musical sounds in the Walsh household.

John had been in good spirits since his chat with Joanna. He was in full swing now and was sure he could complete his book before the Christmas holidays. He was describing the Indian countryside in the exact terms with which Wordsworth wrote about the English countryside. He remembered all the sonnets and the lovely English countryside where he and Joanna had spent many nights wandering in the meadows on starlit nights with crescent moons. Crescent moons and stars have different significance for different ethnicities.

He glanced out of the window and spotted the grand old lady already out in the yard giving instructions to Jose and the priest as how to lay the bricks for the altar for the anniversary of the deaths of Mamta, Seshi, Sunny, and Rammayya garu.

This was one ritual the grand old lady insisted they perform. Only a few guests had been invited. They had been close to Mamta, the kids, and the grand old man. The munsab from the village was always sent a ticket and flown in for this day for the past two years. Joanna, John, and their kids were always there. The old woman used to say that they were her Seshi and Sunny. The bond between them was one that no one could have ever imagined. I guess God strips you of some bondage and you create new bondages. Ever since Seshi had left the house, Boss Man's daughter Mary had become a part and parcel of the Rao family. Rohit always saw his Mamta in her and she loved the family with all her heart and started to despise her father and uncle for their behavior. She preached that differences have to be understood and should not be exaggerated to suit one's own belief. She claimed that everything is a belief. Belief is never a perfect truth, since belief is only what you want to believe in as the absolute truth. She took to pursuing the absolute truth.

She claimed that everything she saw could be negated by a rational thought process. That which can be negated cannot be absolute truth. She felt it was a very thorny journey she was on. On Rohit's advice she had started medical school. Boss Man felt that if any good had come out of that disbeliever Hindu, it was that it was his daughter going to medical school.

Disbeliever of what? God?

John and Joanne's kids loved Grandma. She told them little stories and answered all their questions. They loved sitting with her at the lakeside and hearing her tell stories. They were surprised at how much she knew. They did not realize that she had earned a Master of Arts degree from Madras University when it had still been run by the British before independence was declared. She never mentioned it to anyone. For that matter, even Rohit did not know.

Joanna summoned John, shouting, "John, breakfast is ready."

"Angel, I will be down in a minute."

"Wake the kids up and ask them to come too."

"OK Angel."

"We're up, Mom. Grandma wants us to be there bright and early."

"Your breakfast is on the table, I have to get dressed." So saying, Joanna left the kitchen and went up the stairs. John was just coming down. They stopped and hugged. "Everything is on the table," she said.

"OK Angel."

"Don't forget to take your medicine."

"I won't."

He came down, sat at the table, opened the *Cleveland Herald,* and frantically searched for an article on Mamta. He did not find any. He was disappointed.

"Dad, what counts is we remember," said Abe.

"Dad, I miss Aunty and Seshi very much; she was like my own sister," said Rose. "She was there for me all the way."

"Three years and people forget."

"Yes dear, short memories." Joanna had joined them.

"The only way we will snap out of this is to visit the place where it all started. Maybe we all should visit Stratford."

"Yes, that would be a change," Joanne agreed.

"I would be able to finish my book and finalize the deal with that company in New York."

"Isn't that the company Aunty suggested?" asked Rose.

"Yes, Mamta's close friends in Wisconsin. Their daughter has just started interning with this company."

"Even after three years she still looks after us, Dad," said Abe.

"Abe…there are only few people in this world like Mamta. She was always living for others."

"Grandma said she was going to translate what the priest chants today. She said it was one of the Upanishads."

"Did you know Upa means connected and also means under. Ni means beneath, and shad means sitting."

"Upa means connected," repeated Rose.

"Ni means beneath," said Abe

"Shad means sitting," said Rose

John concluded, "All put together, it means sitting connected at the feet of a master. For instance, Jesus went up the mountain and disciples followed him and sat at his feet to listen to his sermon. They were connected. Upanishad is a treatise on seeking truth."

"When were they written?" asked Abe.

"It is said they were passed on by word of mouth for a long time, for at least few hundred years, before they were actually penned in Sanskrit, somewhere between 800 B.C. and 600 B.C."

"Grandma speaks very good English," said Rose.

"She has a post-graduate degree in literature," Joanne informed them.

"Go away!" Abe and Rose exclaimed

"I didn't know about it, till Mamta mentioned it to me once on my trip to India. She told me because I had been talking to Grandma very slowly in English, as if I was trying to make her understand—you know what I mean."

"We know Mom, sometimes you do that with us."

"Kidding aside, she told me that Grandma won a gold medal for being at the top of her school."

"Really?"

"Yes, Aunty Mamta kept her medal in her prayer room."

"Oh," said Abe. "We saw that and we wondered what a British coat of arms was doing in their prayer room."

"Mamta used to say that it always reminded her of being very humble even though you have accomplished a lot. She said that kept her on an even keel."

"So I will book your tickets to go to Stratford with the kids," said John

"OK."

"On your return we will go to Disney."

"Yeah! That would be great!" shouted the kids.

"Aren't you getting old for that?" kidded John.

"There is no age for Disney, Dad," said Abe.

Joanne stood up from the table. "It's getting late, let's finish and scoot."

"Yes we don't want to miss the story," said John.

They finished their breakfast and started across the backyard lawn towards the place where the homa[10] was being built. Abe, Rose, and Mary, who joined them from the house, went and hugged Grandma and then inspected the intricate way the bricks were being placed. Grandma was sitting on a lawn chair and there was a picnic table where all the children could sit.

The priest came and started to get things ready. John, Joanna, and Rohit watched the happenings from the big bay window.

"I don't want to miss the story," said Joanne.

"Neither do I," said John.

"Grandma said she would come inside no sooner the ritual begins," Rohit told them. "She said it wouldn't disturb the priest and she can tell us the meaning in peace with his chanting in the background."

---

10 A ritual fire

Outside, Grandma got up and started to walk towards the house with the children. Mary raced ahead and arranged an easy chair for her near the bay window. Everyone was always anxious to hear her stories and this was a dandy one.

The fire was started and more arrangements were made. Jose had arranged a hose to make sure that there was water, just in case. Rohit had gotten permission from the fire chief for what he said was a campfire.

"Grandma, please tell the story," said Mary.

"This is not going to be a story but a kind of quiz first."

"Do I get million dollars if I'm right?" laughed Abe.

"You will get a million dollars' worth of knowledge. How about that? Children, please go get your pop and munchies so we can concentrate."

The fridge was raided and the pop and munchies were taken out. Mary, who always took care of Grandma, brought her a stainless steel pitcher of water and a glass.

The children were ready. So were the adults. Jose came in to inform them that the priest was ready.

"Jose, when we are ready you can tell him to start," said Grandma.

Jose, who had gotten used to her style of running the house, understood and he just waited for further instructions and to hear what story she'd tell. He loved her stories too. Everyone was anxious.

Seethamma finally began. "Children, what are three elements that can defy gravity?"

"Gravity?"

"The pull from the earth."

The children scratched their heads. Abe put one and one together and deduced that since there was fire in the brick altar, that could be one answer. "Fire," he said.

"Yes and why?"

Abe had not expected this turn of events. He made a face, threw his arms up and said, "It was a guess, Grandma."

"Wind, air, breeze," Mary offered.

"Light," added Rose.

"In India, before the advent of written history…"

Rose interrupted. "What's that?"

"A long time ago, before people started to write on palm leaves."

"Say 5000 years ago," added Rohit.

"Yes, it was then people in India said that if fire, air, and light are the three elements that can defy gravity, one can send messages to the Universe, using these three as vehicles."

"I get it," said Rose. "Like your own long-distance line to the Universe."

Mary was curious. "Why to the Universe?"

"Because they felt that somewhere in the far Universe lay the secret of who God really is."

"Aren't there different gods?" enquired Abe.

"I don't know, but he has to be same for everyone."

"Then why do people do those ugly things like blow up planes and kill people?" This was a pointed question from Abe. He was the youngest in the group and had no inhibitions. He said and asked what came to his mind. He did not know what it is to manipulate an individual thinking process through psychological gymnastics.

"Abe, you don't ask such questions." Rose was trying to spare Seethamma from answering the question.

Seethamma was not disturbed. "You are talking about your dear friend Sunny, aren't you?"

There were tears in Abe's eyes. Sunny had been his very good friend. It wasn't only the adults who had been close, the kids were close as well. "I miss him, Grandma."

"That's why it is good for people to feel comfortable in talking their thoughts out, though they should never insist that others have to follow their route. There is no absolute truth in this creation. There is what is called relative truth."

Abe wiped his tears. "What is relative truth?"

"It is something like Einstein's theory of relativity. Everything we do is relative to some other thing. If that other thing did not exist, the original presumption becomes invalid."

Abe understood. "You are saying the belief of those who placed the bomb on the plane was the relative other thing."

"Precisely."

"If they did not exist or did not insist that their thought process was right, but only followed it by themselves, then we would have Sunny with us."

"You are getting the hang of it."

"But…But…Sunny, Seshi, and Aunty Mamta had nothing to do with their fight. Aunty Mamta was the best. She loved and helped. She would never fight with anyone; she was too cool."

They all had moist eyes except for the grand old lady. She was very pragmatic. She never let anything get her down. She always said there was a superior purpose for every living creature, though they clutter their brains with trivial pursuits and beliefs. "That's the problem with the world," she said. "Everyone thinks what they believe is perfect."

"If God is really God he would not discriminate would he?" asked Mary.

"No he would not."

"Sorry Grandma, it was bothering me," she said. "You were saying, 5000 years ago in India…"

"The Rishis felt that it was through fire, wind, and light they would be able to communicate with the nether regions of the Universe."

It dawned on Abe. "That's why the priest is making the fire at the altar."

"Now I will tell you a story, which was in one of the ancient Upanishads called Katha Upanishad. Jose, ask the priest to start the ceremony."

Jose ran down, asked the priest to start, and then came back as soon as he could so as not to miss the story.

"Many thinkers in the past contemplated various issues mankind was facing. Each one considered an issue and wrote a treatise, which was taught to his students. These were initially memorized by the students and got verbally passed on from generation to generation. It was when the script was developed it was put on palm leaves and recorded, which was about 5000 BC. Really, no one knows when they were conceived or in many cases by whom."

That intrigued John. "So you are saying no one knows who the author really is."

"Yes. Today is the third anniversary. I have asked the priest to recite Katha Upanishad. This specifically deals with the subject of death…"

Everyone wanted their two cents worth in the discussion.

"What are you going tell us about death?" asked Mary.

"Me tell you? No way."

"Then what?" Joanna asked

"The story is as mentioned in Katha Upanishad."

"Mom, she is translating what the priest is saying in Sanskrit."

"Yes and the story is…"

Outside, the priest chanted in Sanskrit as a fire burned in the pit.

The old woman told the story. "Once upon a time there was a householder in ancient India by the name Vaga-Sar-Vasa. He had a son named Nachiketa. Desirous of a place in Heaven and the rewards associated with it, Vaga-Sar-Vasa surrendered all that he possessed as a sacrifice…"

"You are telling us what the priest is chanting?" asked Rose.

"I am telling the story in an Americanized form, so it is easy to understand. It gives you an idea of the philosophy behind it."

Abe was curious. "Then what?"

Grandma continued. "Nachiketa felt that not only was his father old but that all he processed was antiquated. The cows were barren, old, and feeble, and were unable to give any milk."

Abe was rapt. "They were useless, in effect."

"Yes. Nachiketa felt that this kind of sacrifice would be reward less and figuring that his father was giving up all his possessions, he wanted to know to whom he was going to be given."

Abe was concerned. "Oh no. He asked his father to whom he was being given? To whom did he give him?"

"When Nachiketa pestered his father, in disgust Vaga-Sar-Vasa said, 'I shall give you to the Lord of Death.' Having said that, the father was now in a bind to fulfill his word for the sacrifice."

"So what did he do? Put him in the fire?"

"No, those were the days when morality ruled the world. Morals were universal—the same for everyone. They did not have any conflicts. There was an universal quest for God Almighty."

"You are saying they were figuring out who really was God," mused Abe.

"No one knew what death was. They did not know what was after death, and neither did they know where they had come from before birth."

"Even now we don't know." Abe turned to John. "Do we, Dad?"

Seethamma continued. "Nachiketa said, 'I am ready to die before all who still have to die. I will go along with those who are in the process of dying. I will find out what is the work of the God of Death. " And taking leave of his family, he set out to find Death."

Mary spoke up. "There are so many who have died in the past, and many who are close to it, and many to follow. Someone who is born has to die. It looks like there is only one truth in this world, which is that anything that is born has to die ultimately."

Everyone looked at Mary in a kind of awe. It was such a high thought process at such a young age.

Seethamma went on. "Nachiketa reached the abode of Death. There was no one to receive him. He was a Brahmin."

"What does that mean?" asked Rose.

"One who is in quest of Brahman, which is God."

"You are saying an American can be a Brahmin?"

"Anyone who is in quest of God. No matter what color, race, ethnicity, or geographical location, or for that matter, universal location."

"You are saying like people on Mars?" asked Abe.

"Wherever in the universe. One who searches for God is usually considered a pious person and should be revered, respected, and given hospitality. He has an inner fire that can consume everything by a mere thought process. He becomes one with God as soon as he finds Him."

"Wow!" exclaimed the three children and the adults thought *Wow* without saying it aloud. You know they were adults, who are inhibited about acknowledging ignorance.

"You are saying that there was no one there to give him coffee," said Mary.

Everyone laughed, coffee, tea, been there done that.

"Yes, there was no hospitality given to him for three days. In Indian culture, people pride themselves on their hospitality. A guest is fed before the householder eats. But in the abode of the Lord of Death, there was no hospitality. One who does not respect one's guest is cursed."

"Uh oh…I can see he's in trouble," said Rose.

"Yes, the Lord of Death came home to find Nachiketa waiting for three days without any hospitality, not even a glass of water. To protect himself from the wrath of a Brahmin, the Lord of Death offered Nachiketa three boons."

"What did he ask for?" asked Abe.

"Firstly, he wanted his father not to be angry with him and to receive him with love when he got back from the abode of the Lord of Death."

"Did he get it?"

"Hold your horses, Abe." Rose was getting angry

"He was favored with his desire. Then for the next he asked, 'In Heaven there is no fear, death, old age, hunger, thirst, or sorrow, and everyone rejoices there. You know the fire sacrifice, which leads us to Heaven and immortality. Tell me and teach me. This I ask of you as my second boon.'

"Yama, Lord of Death, explained to Nachiketa the ritual of the fire sacrifice that leads one to eternal life. He said fire was the beginning of all the worlds. Even Earth was a ball of fire before it cooled down. He explained the method with which one should perform this sacrifice. He who performs this three times is united with father, mother, and teacher, and he who has performed three duties of study, sacrifice, and alms-giving is rid of the chains of death. Yama further said, 'I give you another boon. From this day forward, the fire sacrifice shall be called Nachiketa Fire. It's your fire that will lead mortals to Heaven.'"

The old woman concluded, "That's what he is doing for the third time in the name of Mamta, Seshi, and Sunny."

"Now I get it, Grandma," said Abe. "But what did he ask for the third boon?"

"Nachiketa said, 'There is doubt, when one is dead. Some say he is and some say he is not. I would like to know the secret.' That is what he asked for his third boon.

"Yama answered, 'On this point even some demi gods have doubted. It is not easy to understand. The subject is delicate and subtle. Choose another boon.'

"Nachiketa answered him back saying, 'If that is the case and it is not easy to understand, with you, the Lord of Death, as my teacher, I would like to receive the understanding of the secret.'

"This was a secret that the Lord of Death did not want to part with. So he tried to tempt Nachiketa with a bribe, and he said, 'Ask an equal boon. Wealth. Long life. Ask to be a king of Earth. I can make you enjoyer of all desires. Ask for difficult desire that mortals long for: beautiful girls like models, chariots, musical instruments, or anything else, but do not ask me about the secret of death.'

"But Nachiketa was not to be bribed. 'These things you offer last only a short while. As youthful vigor wears out so do all the senses. Life is short. Keep your horses, girls, and temptations to yourself. No man is made happy by wealth. Shall we continue to be rich when we encounter you? How can we be everlasting as long as you are there and would summon us to die? Mortals decay and would wish to know and delight in long life after having pondered on all the pleasures of this mortal body, beauty and love. The doubt on death is what I need to know. Tell me what is there after death. That's the boon I ask from you.'"

"Did he tell the truth behind death?" This came from Joanna and she added, "Last night we saw a light that we think was Mamta."

"Did you?" asked Rohit. "The only thing I know is it has appeared every year at the same time for the past three years. So logically it has to be…" He couldn't complete his sentence as he choked. He cleared his throat and rubbed his moist eyes.

Grandma smiled and continued the story. "God is an individual's personal perception. It is unique like a fingerprint. Just like there are no identical snowflakes, every individual's perception of God is unique to him or her. It's their personal space. Each one has to make peace with their perception of God. So I am going to tell the answer as is and will let you make your own judgments and perceptions of what is said."

"Grandma. Are you running for the Senate?" cracked Mary.

Everyone laughed and they needed a laugh, believe me.

"Good and pleasant are poles apart. He who chooses pleasant misses his end. Both approach us. The wise choose good and the unwise choose pleasant through greed and avarice.

"Imagine you have dismissed pleasant. You did not choose the road to wealth and riches. Ignorance and what is known as wisdom, are two thought processes that lead to two different destinations. If you are a follower of wisdom, then pleasures do not tempt you. When the wise man rests his mind in contemplation of God beyond time, who invisibly dwells in the mystery of things and in the heart of man, he rises above pleasures and sorrows.

"If the slayer thinks that he kills and the slain thinks that he dies, neither knows the ways of truth. The eternal in man cannot kill and the eternal in man cannot die. Concealed in all beings is the spirit, the self, smaller than the smallest sub-atom, and greater than the vast spaces.

"When the wise realize the omnipresent Spirit, who rests invisible in the visible and permanent in the impermanent, then they go beyond sorrow. Not through learning is he reached, not through intellect and teaching. It is reached by His chosen, and it is because they choose Him. To His chosen he reveals His glory.

"Unless evil ways are abandoned, there is rest in the senses, concentration in the mind, and peace in one's heart, that's when one can reach the glorious spirit.

"Know the Lord as the charioteer, and the body as the chariot.

"Know that reason is the charioteer, and the mind indeed is the reins. The horses, they say, are the senses and their paths are the objects of senses.

"One who has not the right understanding, and whose mind is never steady, is not the ruler of his life. He is like an intoxicated driver with wild horses. Right understanding with a steady mind makes one a ruler of his own destiny, like a good driver with well-trained horses. He who has not the right understanding, is careless and never pure, reaches not the end of the journey, but keeps wandering from pleasure to pleasure and thus from death to death. One whose chariot is driven by reason, who watches and holds the reins of his mind and senses, reaches the end of the journey, the supreme, everlasting Spirit.

"Beyond the spirit in man is the spirit of Universe, and beyond is the Spirit Supreme or what we call God. Nothing is beyond the Spirit Supreme; it's the end of the path.

"This Supreme Spirit is common and the same world over. It is, as I said, personal to each individual and specific to that person only."

"So you are saying my God is what I make out of him," said Abe.

"My God can be different from my mom's," Rose added.

"It's your personal perception of Him that counts, but watch out, you have to respect others' perceptions as well because it's their perception of God. He is omnipresent and omnipotent, so He can be different but is the same at the end of the journey."

"I get it, Grandma—all Gods are the same with different names," said Mary.

"This is a synopsis of what he was chanting," finished the old woman.

Joanna sounded thoughtful. "You are telling me that even though they think they have slain, really they have not, in a broader sense."

"Yes Joanna, this gives us closure on the issue of death."

"What happened to Nachiketha?" asked John.

"Oh! He got the knowledge and went back to his father's house. He lived a life in quest of the supreme self within, with a mind that was guided by reason, and…"

"Like a good driver with well-trained horses." This from the youngest in the audience concluded the grand old lady's story. Everyone got up and hit the dining table for their sumptuous lunch.

At this point in the narration, the group at RSL Productions also took a break for lunch. Bob volunteered to pay for it. That was a change, and Priya and Simrin shared glances. As usual, Bob got an early start and started down the steps. The other three took the elevator and stood outside to wait for him on the steps in front of the building. As soon as they saw him, they started to walk down.

"What does your palate feel like? Tell me, the treat is on me."

"It doesn't matter," said John. "Something close by."

"You must like fish and chips, there is a good British restaurant."

"It's lunch time, a good fast-food restaurant should be fine."

Priya butted-in with her two cents worth. "Tomorrow we start our ten-day vacation."

Bob was insistent. "You have to promise me that you will let me buy you a really good big meal in one of those posh restaurants,"

"Sure," said John, "once we have finalized the deal and signed."

"That's a done deal with what I have heard so far."

Priya and Simrin were stunned. This was the first time that Bob had been that impressed with anyone. This had really gotten him going. First, taking them out to lunch, then a big dinner, and accepting a proposal even before it was completed. No negotiation—this took the cake.

As the two were wondering, the cell phone rang and Bob answered, "Hi darling…just a minute." Looking at Priya and Simrin, he said, "It's Betty, I need to talk to her. You go ahead and get the orders. Priya, you pick up the bill and put it in your expense account, OK?"

As Priya and others were walking away to McDonald's, he called out, "Priya get me a McFillet and fries with a Diet Coke."

"OK, will do."

They walked to the McDonald's, placed their orders and sat inside waiting for Bob while watching him outside talking with Betty.

"It must be mid-night over there."

"No Simrin, it would be a six-hour difference. Must be early morning."

John said, "It is precisely a five-hour difference from New York. It's twelve-noon here and it will be five in the evening there."

"Isn't it funny that Bob seems to be talking to Betty a lot more than usual?" Priya asked Simrin. "He always used to say he was busy. Now he can't seem to stop talking to her. That's a change in his behavior."

"Yes, just wait and see, he'll send her kisses on the phone."

They both suddenly realized they were in PG's company and they looked sick about having said this in front of him.

PG smiled in a kind of *I know what you guys are thinking*-way and said, "Doesn't love have a weird way of getting people to realize what they're missing? You know it gives them a chance to make-up lost time."

As PG was saying that, Bob was kissing Betty good-bye and then he joined them in the restaurant. To Priya and Simrin's surprise he said, "PG, that was my wife, Betty. She is on vacation in England with my two kids, Sam and Suzie."

PG smiled with a hint of wetness in his eyes. What Bob said next actually floored Priya and Simrin, but neither of them let it show. "I love them, PG. I love them, my wife, my son, and Suzie."

"I understand…"

"PG you're a writer, tell me, why do men get that seven-year-itch?"

Priya joined in the conversation. "You mean seven, fourteen, twenty-one, twenty-eight?"

Simrin put a face that asked Priya, *Are you out of your freakin' mind?*

Unconscious, Bob countered, "I've only been married twenty-one years. The bachelor life and juices take control in a cyclic pattern, I suppose, just like the Wall Street cycles."

This was the first time Bob had started to talk about his personal life without being inhibited and as if he had nothing to hide. This was a significant change at least from the vantage point of Simrin and Priya. Who else would have known him? It looked like PG's story had had an effect on him for sure.

They finished the meal and started back to the office. The clock on the street corner showed 12:45.

The late August sun was blasting on the people of New York. There was a slight breeze from the south. It was cool and made everyone comfortable. People were eating their mid-day lunches on the steps of the office buildings. There were people just soaking up the sun with gay abandon. Young lovers smooched on the street corners. There was the sense of free birds just enjoying themselves, completely unaware of their surroundings. Freedom, prosperity, full employment, and stability were evident at every corner in this magnificent city of New York. Everyone was looking forward to what the glorious future had in store for them. Children were getting ready to get back to school after their summer holidays. Preparations for the Labor Day parade were in full swing.

PG and the others got back to the office and reconvened in the conference room to let PG start his narration again.

Chapter Nineteen

PG put up a storyboard with a date, as he started the narration. And it was...

December 21st, 1988. 16:00:00 GMT.
Joanna and the kids checked in, passed through the British customs line, and entered the secure area of London's Heathrow Airport. The kids hit the duty-free shops. Abe bought himself a Cadbury milk chocolate bar. Rose hit the cosmetics. Joanna hit the shop that sold men's ties. She found a tie with elephants on it, bought it for John and had it wrapped with a bow attached. The sales girl asked, "Do you want to include a card for your boyfriend?"

"What makes you think he is my boyfriend?"

"Isn't that what all Americans do?"

In Europe they think American society is promiscuous. In the U.S., we are a poll-driven society. Polls can slant your conclusions every which way you want them to. American movies tend to show quick endings to relationships without the long, drawn-out romance, unless it is a romantic movie. These give the Europeans something to point fingers at.

"What makes you think I am an American?"

"Your jeans."

Joanna had had enough of this. Changing her accent completely to the British style from Stratford, she said, "I was born here near Stratford on the banks of the Avon. Do you know what the Avon is?"

The sales girl was taken aback and muttered, "Cosmetics."

"It's a famous river."

"Hum."

"Don't stereotype Americans, they have more values than most people in Europe."

"Hum."

"He is my husband, and yes I would like to include a card."

"Hum."

"Is it too late?"

The salesgirl looked at the wrapped gift. "For you, not at all, I will wrap it again. Please take this card and write your message."

As she was undoing the wrapping, Joanna wrote the message and gave her the card. The salesgirl inserted the message into the box and re-wrapped the box again. Joanna had a habit of sticking her name labels, which had been sent to her by the American Cancer Society, on all her letters and messages. She stuck one on this message also. It was her way of remembering her father who died of cancer.

The kids joined her as the sales girl was retracting her earlier statements to her about Americans.

Abe and Rose had their own version of that. They felt it was a jealous point of view that Europeans used to get at Americans. They knew it wasn't true but wanted to believe that it was.

The three moved to the gate as the Boeing 747-121 rolled in from Frankfurt. The gate agent announced in an English accent, "Flight 103 has just arrived from Frankfurt. The flight to New York will depart on time. We will start the boarding process as soon as the crew cleans the aircraft for its Trans-Atlantic flight."

Flight 103 took off from Heathrow Airport at 6.25. It took a 350-degree heading and flew at a 600-foot elevation. It then got clearance, climbed to 12,000 feet, and subsequently leveled off at 31,000 feet. The time was 6:56 in the evening, Greenwich Mean Time.

Ironically, Priya glanced at the clock on the wall in the conference room and it read 1:56 in the afternoon. That was exactly the same time as that day on Dec 21st 1988. It sent a chill down her back and she reacted to it.

Simrin saw what was happening to Priya. She looked at the clock and understood what it meant. The same chill went down her back.

Bob noticed a teardrop trickle down PG's cheek. He didn't know what to make of this guy. He commented to himself that PG would make a good actor. He felt he had what it took for a Shakespearean actor to flourish in the tragedies.

Joanne and the kids were seated in the middle seats. They were in very high spirits because they were going to Disney as soon as they landed in New York.

"I can't wait to get back and see, Dad," said Rose.

"Neither can I."

"I miss him too," Joanne said. "This is the first time we have been separated since that trip to India."

"Mom, why do I still miss Sunny?"

"I miss Seshi too."

"Because they are your good friends."

"No, I have many other friends but no one like Sunny."

"Me too, but Seshi."

"My friendship with Mamta was similar."

The three of them just sat there reminiscing and trying to figure out why.

"I've got it," said Joanne.

"What Mom?"

"They are from a civilization that is thousands of years old," said Joanne, as she thought about the Hindu way of life. "They were a peace-loving civilization. They were invaded again and again by many foreigners. The Hindu way of life taught them to respect other's convictions. They have all along absorbed the good from the invaders and let them stay there without rebelling. This non-oppressive stance of their: the civilization was taken for granted. The power was grabbed and then the oppressors started conversions at knifepoint and through intimidation. In some cases, they bribed the Hindus to convert."

"How can God discriminate between people? Aren't they all his children?" asked Abe.

"God loves everyone. He doesn't show favoritism."

"I once asked Sunny why he prayed to an idol."

"What did he say?"

"He said it helped him concentrate more. He said his brain was like a monkey, always trying to jump hither and thither."

"It leads us into temptation," said Rose.

"That's why we say lead us not into temptation—it's the same thing," said Joanne.

"That's what we concluded in the end, Mom."

"I wish everyone was as wise as you children are."

"Like the story of Leo Tolstoy."

"What?" Joanna was surprised that Abe had read anything by Tolstoy.

"I saw this book in Sunny's room," he said. "Short stories from around the world. This story got my attention."

"You mean this Tolstoy story."

"Yes. "Little Children are Wiser than Men." It had a moral."

"What was it?"

"You have to resolve conflicts and get together instead of fighting. Like children forgive and forget."

"Your dad would be so proud of you if you told him this."

The three of them hugged each other.

In cargo bay 14L, below where they were sitting, there was a small Toshiba stereo boom box, marketed and available only in the Middle East and northern Africa. Undiscovered in the security checks, it had a two-step detonator. The first was a barometer-detonator that triggered with low pressure. The second was a timer and as soon as the higher altitude of over 25,000 feet was reached, it started to tick silently in the cargo hold.

Time, which has a tendency not to stop for anyone, was merrily ticking away without anyone knowing what was ahead, The time was…

19 Hours: 02 Minutes: 50 Seconds Greenwich Mean Time.

This time, Priya, Simrin, Bob, and PG all looked at the clock on the wall in the conference room. The second hand was ticking from 48 to 49 to 50. There was silence in the room. It lasted for a while. Everyone's thoughts traveled at phenomenal speeds. They were contemplating how fragile life is and how it is exploited by the rule-following and unruly as well.

There was a violent explosion in the 14L cargo hold. The main electronic center of the plane was damaged so the radios to send distress signals were destroyed. The outer skin of the aircraft started to glow as if it was being subjected to a very high temperature just below the belly of the giant Boeing 747 plane. It looked like some evil force was trying to mold the future of human existence. At the same time, the red-hot aluminum metal was exposed to the sub-zero temperatures of the higher altitude. I guess this is what is called Hell. Hell as in Christian theology. Hell as in Jewish theology. Hell as in Buddhist theology. Hell as in Hindu theology. Hell as in Mayan theology. Hell as in Islamic theology.

The metal was quenched.

Hot explosive gases pierced through the aluminum metal structure and formed small perforations. Simultaneously there was a ghastly explosion that sent thousands and thousands of fragments of the fuselage and anything around it hurtling outward at speeds in excess of a thousand feet per second. Anything that travels at this speed and velocity is as deadly as a bullet.

Air traffic control in Prestwick, Scotland, was tracking the progress of Flight 103 to New York at its 31,000-foot altitude, just south of the border of Scotland. The plane was very close to the city of Lockerbie. Suddenly the one blip of the tracking screen changed and became four very bright blips. They flashed bright on the radar screen. Then the screen went dark and blank.

The tremendous blast shattered a twenty-foot by twenty foot hole. The fuselage skin ruptured and the pressure impulses quickly spread to the whole body of the plane. The belly of the plane was the first to give way, followed by total disintegration.

Within seconds, all the contents of the plane began to fall to the ground in pieces along with the bodies of its 259 passengers. The fuselage and the wings separated. The nose cone and the wings started their descent as if to defy fate and landed on a street in the city of Lockerbie. In the process they scraped the tops of houses and set them on fire. Lockerbie's Sherwood Crescent was the worst hit. The inferno from the crash set ablaze in excess of twenty buildings and destroyed them beyond repair. There were eleven unfortunate victims on the ground, who did not realize what hit them. Debris flew all around and the neighborhood looked like an inferno.

Pillows, life jackets, chunks of metal, and body parts of the victims were scattered over a thousand square miles.

In Lockerbie there was a crater 155 feet wide and 196 feet long. It looked like a huge grave for Flight 103.

From its stations in the north just bordering Scotland, the British Geological Survey recorded a seismic event measuring 1.6 on the Richter scale.

Against the blue background of the Scottish sky was a long, wrapped red box with a blue bow floating away at 25,000 feet in the air.

It landed, ironically, in front of a United Kingdom Royal Mail Post Office, requesting to be delivered. It was a faraway cry from a lover who had missed her debonair husband. It lay there screaming for someone to pick-up and deliver it. It had a Christmas ring to it. It had a subliminal message of Peace on Earth.

Mr. McLaughlin was on his way to see the commotion of the 747 landing on the street and the havoc it had caused. He spotted the package in front of the post office, picked it up, and examined it. Immediately, he knew it must be something that had fallen from the plane. He felt an unexpected urge to keep it safe and wait for the right moment.

What moment? He was confused. His mind was playing tricks on him. Why was it telling him things that didn't make sense? He was trying to make logical sense of his behavior. Does a pot of gold under the rainbow make sense? Does a leprechaun make sense? Does Brigadoon make sense?

Suddenly his mind sent another vibe that was spine chilling. Does one's individual, personal God make sense?

He approached the scene of the disaster. The first thought that crossed his mind was, how could God allow this kind of atrocity to take place? Why does he let people portray him as a benefactor for the few and as an angry, absolutely ruthless entity for the other? If he is so great, why does he let some unfortunate soul be born in a downtrodden place while someone else starts his life with a golden spoon in his hand? If God allows this to happen at random, is there any logic associated with all this helter skelter, muddled interpretation of the entity called God?

Granted, some say God speaks to them. Invariably, these are the guys that instigate and propagate atrocities all over the world. The more Mr. McLaughlin tried to make sense of all the things that were happening in this small town of Lockerbie in remote Scotland, the more it became absolutely impossible for him to understand. Super-imposed on this mosaic, his mind started to review the Christian faith and its multifarious denominations. He assessed the Islamic faith too and realized it was no different with Sunnis,

Shiites and many others. It looked like wherever there are people, there was going to be strife, coupled with dogmatic beliefs and for some reason an insatiable thirst to convert everyone else to another's way of thinking. I guess in the end, if they cannot convince others to accept that they are right, it probably negates their own thought process. That which that cannot be negated is the absolute truth.

Mr. McLaughlin said out loud in his Scottish accent, "I sure hope we can find the absolute truth, but we will have a hell of a time getting people to accept it."

He came to the disaster zone and could not stomach it, so he turned back, threw up on the side of the road, and went home. He sat on his favorite chair with the package on the table and he stared at it. He was trying to sense what stories it had hidden behind it.

The swinging doors of a tall building on Wall Street opened and out emerged John, with a big smile on his face. He gave a panhandling homeless guy a dollar and proceeded to the corner payphone, where he dialed a number and waited for the phone to be picked-up.

"Hello John, you made it, did you?"

"Grandma, how did you know?"

"Well you let me read it, didn't you?"

"I did."

"Do you know I read a lot of literature?"

"Yes I do."

"Comparatively, your writing is good and should be given a chance."

"So you think everyone else will think like you?"

"Anyone with a good head on his shoulders should think the same way. When you read the contemporary novelists, you will find yours a treat to read and it has human interest in it too."

"Grandma, thanks for your encouragement."

"Don't forget Joanna. She is your lucky charm. Behind every man there is a woman who holds the fort. She is the one who makes things happen."

"You are right, Grandma."

"So what is the news? It's your turn to brag."

In the background John heard, "Who is it, Grandma?."

"Rohit it is John, he has some good news."

"Let me put him on the speaker." Rohit switched the phone to speaker mode. "Hey buddy, what's up?"

"That's supposed to be my line."

"That's OK, you are a doctor of arts, John."

"What's up Doc?"

"John you did not sell them any rights as yet, did you?"

"No, not yet, they're preparing a letter of intent for me to review and they may want me to sign it tomorrow."

"John, don't sign anything till our attorney here sees it and approves it. The entertainment guys are too slick for us commoners."

"I was planning to let Joanna see it and approve it first."

"I just got a call from her an hour ago, as they were waiting to board the plane at Heathrow. She and kids cannot wait to see you. They are excited about the Disney trip."

"I'm going to Times Square for a while, and then I'll head off to JFK on the airport bus to meet them at 8.30."

"Great, what did they offer for the book?"

"The details are going to be in that 'intent' document."

"Are they giving you an advance?"

"Yes, they are. They're going to tell me the exact amount tomorrow and they kind of hinted that they may give me a check for that amount."

"Good, let's be cool and maybe negotiate a good deal for you."

"OK you're the boss in commercial dealings."

"John, I cannot wait to see you," interjected Seethamma.

"Neither can I, Grandma. I couldn't have done it without your help and proofreading."

"I get a plug in the foreword."

"What do you mean a plug? You can write the foreword."

"I love you, John."

"I love you, Grandma…Talk to you later, Rohit."

"OK. Take care of yourself."

John hung up the phone feeling like he had given birth to something very special. He saw a corner shop, went in, and asked for a Cuban Corona Special cigar.

"They are banned."

"Do I look like a customs officer or NYPD?"

"No."

"Then what's the problem?"

"I don't carry them."

Just then, one of the customers paid his bill and walked out of the store.

"What do you mean that you don't carry them?"

"Hold your horses, the guy who was shopping there is an inspector, and I can't give you Cuban cigars, they're banned here. You know that."

"Yes I do know that and also that at least eighty percent of the smoke shops carry them."

"What's the occasion, did you close a deal?"

"Yes. I sold my story to a producer. He wants to sign the contract tomorrow. It's like my baby has been born."

"This one is on me."

"Thanks! Once I have sold it for sure, I'll take you out to dinner."

"OK, it's a deal."

John left the shop and started to walk toward Times Square, a very popular place to visit in New York for the tourists and the locals as well. John was going there to catch the bus to JFK.

On his way he saw a crowd gathered near a sidewalk newsstand and got a queer feeling in his stomach. He felt uneasy. All kinds of emotions were haunting him. He thought it was the Cuban cigar he was smoking. As he came up to the crowd, his anxiety started to build. He walked up to the crowd and asked someone, "What's happening?"

"CNN."

"CNN what?"

"Breaking news." The guy was irritated.

John had no time for that, so he started to walk towards Times Square. His stomach-turning did not stop, so he had a piece of spearmint gum, though he continued to smoke his cigar.

Another crowd had gathered at the next newsstand where there was a TV screen, and he stopped again to enquire, "What's the news about?"

"Flight 103 from London to JFK crashed."

"Did you say Flight 103?"

"Yes."

John pushed people aside and went to the front to watch the news on CNN. The CNN anchor was retelling the breaking news. "We have it from reliable sources that just minutes after take-off, Flight 103 from London's Heathrow to JFK crashed in Lockerbie, a small town in Scotland. Preliminary reports indicate that there are no survivors. We will keep you posted as the story develops."

A hydrogen bomb exploded in John's heart. It became very heavy. His eyes filled with tears. He grabbed the guy next to him with two hands and looking straight into his eyes asked him pointedly, "Don't tell me it's Flight 103."

"Yes it's 103."

"Don't tell me its Joanna's plane. Joanna, my wife."

The crowd started to understand and sympathize. "It was Pan Am Flight 103," someone said.

"No…No…No!!"

John's grip was getting tight on the man's neck. "Maybe your wife is on another flight."

"Don't tell me Joanna is gone."

"We don't know."

John moved to the next guy there and said, "Don't tell me Joanna is gone."

"We don't know."

John just fell to the ground sobbing and saying, "Don't tell me Joanna is gone."

Continuing to sob…he cried, "Don't tell me Joanna is gone. God can't do this. Where is there a church?"

One of the guys pointed him down the street to a church.

John started to run towards it, crying and on the way saying to everyone he passed, "Don't tell me Joanna is gone."

He got to the church, opened the front door, and entered, then he ran through the pews. At the altar, there was a huge cross with Jesus hanging on it. To one side there was the Virgin Mary.

John lit a candle and looking at Mary's face said, "Don't tell me Joanna is gone."

He moved to the cross and started to shout, "Tell your Father that Joanna is a very Christian lady, who never even hurt a fly. It's not right for Him to take her away. It's not right. It is nature's way for the older to die first and then the young. How come He is changing the rules? What right has He to change it whenever it pleases Him? Does he know how young Rose and Abe are? They haven't even tasted the fruits of life yet. They are like freshly blossomed flowers, and their nectar has not even been shared by the whole world. Their potential has not been explored. Who gave you the right to impose your rules?

"Who gave you the right to enforce regulations on every human being? Is it your whim and fancy? Tell me? Come on, just don't hang there! Tell me! I know, maybe your Father is not the real God. That's why he let you die on the cross. He let those barbarians crucify you. Why am I even talking to you? I should be talking to the real God."

A priest was listening to the whole monologue. He came to comfort John but to no avail. John was convinced he was barking up the wrong tree. He ran out into the street again, saying to the pedestrians, "Don't tell me Joanna is gone. Don't tell me Joanna is gone."

He saw a mosque, immediately ran in, and started to search for some kind of an icon. All he found was a wall. As he looked at the wall he realized it pointed towards Mecca. He kneeled down and started to pray. "Allah, I know I never prayed to you before, but please don't let this happen to Joanna and the kids. They are I have in this world. Without them I have nothing to live for. Take my life instead."

As he was walking out, a man there indicated that he had to cover his head when he prayed and offered him a cap. John got out of there and took off in search of a synagogue. When he found one, he entered the inner prayer room and prayed to God.

"You are older than the others. You are the Old Testament. You probably started this whole system. Then why are you changing the rules? Please help me and make this news not true."

Coming out on to the street again, not knowing what to do, he started to say to everyone, "Don't tell me Joanna is gone. Don't tell me Joanna is gone."

He remembered that there was a Hindu temple in Flushing and set out to go there. Stumbling upon a taxi driver, he said to him, "Don't tell me Joanna is gone."

"Joanna who?"

"My wife."

"Was she on the plane?"

"Don't tell me Joanna is gone."

"Get into my taxi, I'll take you wherever you want."

God works in mysterious ways. John started to wonder and think aloud, "Joanna, did you decide that you would join your friend Mamta? I need to talk to God."

"Which God?" the taxi driver asked.

"Ganesh," John blurted out

"He is right here on my dash."

"Is He not in the temple?"

"God is omnipresent. He is everywhere."

"What do you mean?"

"He is in you. A part of Him is in you."

"I am not God."

"If He is not in you, and you are different than God, then He is not omnipresent and as such is not God."

"You are telling me He is in every one of us?"

"Yes. Seek Him inside yourself."

John closed his eyes and started to pursue this God. He put his palms together and prayed to Him, requesting that He make it not happen. But somewhere there was an irksome feeling that the news was correct and he was battling a lost cause. "Where are you taking me?"

"JFK, to the airline counter; they will have answers for you."

John was exhausted from his battle with God. He literally collapsed in the back seat. The taxi driver brought him to JFK and asked a cop to keep an eye on him while he found out what to do at the counter.

The cop was very helpful under the circumstances. The airline counter clerk suggested that the taxi driver bring John in and leave him with them, so they could make arrangements for him to fly to Lockerbie. John came into the terminal in a daze. The Good Samaritan left him in the care of the airline and went about his chores for the day. There are people who go out of their way to help people.

John came out of his daze and started to say to the airline employees, "Don't tell me Joanna is gone. Don't tell me Joanna is gone."

The airline arranged a charter flight to the United Kingdom and flew it into an airport that was close to Lockerbie. From there they bussed all the kith and kin to the crash site. It was thought the visit there would bring closure to the mental gymnastics one goes through in situations like this.

All through, John was saying to everyone, "Don't tell me Joanna is gone."

The people of Lockerbie tried to be very hospitable. Everyone came to greet the busload of family members of the crash victims.

Mr. McLaughlin was moved to see the families of the victims. He carried the package with him, but he stayed quite aloof for he did not want to get in the way of the grieving families. Everyone was trying to comfort them. John went on his pursuit and started asking each and every one, "Did you see my Joanna, Abe, and dear Rose?" He made sure that he did not miss any one there near the crash site. As he was looking around, he saw a grim old man standing under a tree holding a small package with a bow attached. Slowly, John started to move towards the old man. As he approached, the old man said, "I am McLaughlin."

"Did you see my Joanna, Abe, and dear Rose?"

"Joanna from Cleveland?"

John immediately held him and hugged him. "Yes…Yes, from Cleveland, Joanna Woodward, where is she? Where are my kids, Abe and Rose? Tell me…tell me…"

Mr. McLaughlin didn't know how to react except to hold him tight.

John did not understand why there was silence. "Did you see my Joanna, Abe, and dear Rose?."

Mr. McLaughlin did not know what to say.

"Did you see my Joanna, Abe, and dear Rose?"

"I did not see them."

"How did you know Joanna is from Cleveland?"

"With this." He showed John the small package.

"What?"

"I found it in front of the post office."

John just gazed at him.

"Something told me that I should hold on to this for some reason." He handed the package to John. "Now I know what the reason was—it was for you."

John took the package and saw the return address. As he tore off the wrapping and opened the box, there was the tie with elephants on it and a letter. He slumped onto the ground and as he was opening the letter, started to cry out loud as the truth sank in. "It's only Joanna who would give you something even when she is dying…It's only Joanna who would give you something…It's only Joanna who would give you something even when she is dying…" John opened his letter and started to read it as he wept.

Mr. McLaughlin suddenly couldn't help but join John in crying. The two of them sat and cried under a tree.

Chapter Twenty

August 30th, 2001

It was five o'clock in the evening. There was pin drop silence in the conference room. None of the participants were willing to make a move or a suggestion. Each of them was in his or her own thoughts reviewing what they'd heard.

Inquisitive as usual, Priya was debating in her mind if this was PG's autobiography. She had been part of the initial arrangements for PG's original presentation. She also remembered vaguely an aunty in Cleveland who had been involved in an accident. She did not have the courage to ask PG, lest he go into one of his mood swings. She was sorry that he had not left any chance for her to mold the story to show her talent, but had given her a fait accompli screenplay that was full in every respect. All she had to do was follow the proceedings as they were laid out in the narration and the storyboards.

Bob, on the other hand, was contemplating how he could entice PG to join his staff. He felt PG had a very vivid imagination and a style that was unique and would be very well accepted by the audience. PG also knew what buttons to push to make a story come alive. It was very natural and alive, without superlative nuances. Nowadays no one was able to write pure fiction with a heart-wrenching story line without using all the special effects of car crashes, high-speed chases, and a whole bunch of bungling police detectives. Writers seemed preoccupied with speed, along with psychological perversion and abuse of the weaker sex. They had to have a rape or an explicit sex scene. The older filmmakers could develop a romance in a soft, sophisticated way and use up a good length of celluloid. The new generation in the art wanted to save money and would rather get the lovers into the sack within few seconds. They were done with establishing the intense attraction between the two. It left them a lot more time for car chases and police detectives. The unfortunate side effect of this happened to be that actors and actresses did not to have to know much about acting but they had to have good pelvic moves and a distinct moan/groan faculty. It was no longer the realm of the porn industry but a norm in the industry, sometimes even on the Broadway stage. Bob was convincing himself that he could bribe PG with a fat paycheck, an expense account, and the usual kickbacks in royalties. He could not wait to get him on board, but was scared to approach him on the subject and was thinking about letting Priya and Simrin do the work for him.

Simrin was just too overwhelmed with the whole story. She was imagining how John had dealt with losing Joanne. How much in love the two of them had been. Poor John lost not only his wife but also his two kids. What did the terrorists get out of their act, other than putting a nice God-fearing family into turmoil? Life is so precious and should be left to God to deal with. Humans have no right to interfere with God's designs. She couldn't help but get her eyes wet.

PG sat with his eyes closed. He was remembering his first encounter with Julia and his proposal. He remembered that moonlit night when Julia had helped him with the plot for his story and assured him that his work would be accepted and become a relevant part of history. His eyes were moist, and almost inaudibly, he whispered, "Julia, I miss you, and you were right, I think I made it."

Priya's intuition was right. John was PG and Joanne was Julia. This was not a fiction but the history of two loving families who had perished at the hands of terrorists, who had acted without any logic and hurt innocent victims who had nothing to do with their convictions and agendas.

The silence continued for few more minutes. PG broke it with, "As promised, I have completed it on time."

Priya, who was anxious to get to Chicago, said, "Yes, it's five and we start our vacation tomorrow."

Bob could not resist saying, "Simrin could you make four copies of the screenplay?"

At this abrupt request from Bob, Priya and Simrin looked at each other. PG had not even given permission for the copying of his work. This is never done without the author being given a waiver to sign. The women were worried how PG would react.

PG knew what was going in their heads, and to relieve them of the anxiety, he said, "It's OK Priya…your dad got me to come here because of you… thanks to Aunty Mamta… it's OK. I am not going to shop around; life is too short and fragile."

Bob smiled. "PG, I would not let you shop around. Here is a blank paper and you can write your terms…we want to do what's right for you."

Priya was surprised and so was Simrin.

"The only thing I want is for Priya to direct this," Bob continued. "She understands the spirit behind this story. I have already asked her to direct and Simrin will be associate… No…no…she will produce this."

This came as a surprise to Simrin.

Priya and Simrin contemplated the irony of the situation. They realized that it was a true story and that one of the characters was right in front of them with all the burns and scars of the unfortunate events. They were dealing with someone's grief while they were being given promotions. Suddenly it came to them that this could be a self-serving proposition.

As the thought crossed their minds, it also occurred to Bob what his outburst could be construed as. "This could look like a self-serving move," he said.

PG, Priya, and Simrin were taken aback for the first time since they had known Bob. He had always been ruthless when it came to business dealings. He felt business and heart did not go together. Business had to be ruthless. Everything had a fitness for the purpose. If it didn't exist it should be history. This was a right turn in his philosophy.

Bob continued, "Priya, you have been with this company for fifteen years and have been loyal and hard working. I should have done this a long time ago. I'm sorry, I will make it up to you. Simrin, you have a good relationship with Priya and the two of you will work well together, and I'm sure you will win some awards for us."

Simrin got up and PG handed over the script. She went to make copies. Priya poured herself a coffee while Bob started to converse with PG. "Don't you think that life is very fragile?"

"Hum…"

"Why do we put so much emphasis on our ultra-egos and achievements and the pride associated with them?"

"Our system doesn't teach humility."

"Doggie DOG, isn't it?"

"Eastern philosophy gets at this in depth."

"The universe is a virtual image as seen in a mirror."

"You know the virtual image is not affected by anything that surrounds it, neither does it affect the mirror in which it appears," said PG.

"I see."

"Living a life without being affected by events that surround you and leaving the fruits of your labor to be determined by the universal force become fundamental issues to be dealt with."

"You mean that you have no control over the results?" asked Bob.

"I mean don't anticipate your results, since the chips fall as they please."

"You mean I have no control."

"Sometimes that which we think is in our complete control is not."

"Explain."

"Our circle of influence is what we perceive it to be"

"Yes."

"Are we right?."

Bob thought for a moment. "I don't know."

"When Julia and the kids went to the UK, I was under the impression that I was in complete control of my destiny. This is in spite of being fully aware of what had happened to Rohit. Sometimes circumstances get us to depend on ourselves rather than the Supreme Entity, which we call by different names."

"I get it." Bob did not get it. He thought he did. PG had just revealed it was a true story that had happened to him.

"The results can be fourfold," John went on.

"Four?"

"Yes: What you expected. Less than you expected. More than you expected, and completely contrary to what you expected."

Simrin and Priya walked in with the copies.

"Let's each have a copy and take it with us on our vacation and read it," said Bob to the women.

"What about the fourth copy?"

"Put one in our filing cabinet, so it will be safe. We will be going on vacation for a week and will come back bright and early on the Monday after next week."

Simrin interjected, "It is Priya's birthday on the tenth, the Sunday."

"Happy birthday." Everyone gave her early birthday greetings.

"Where will you celebrate?" asked Bob.

"In Chicago with my parents."

"If you want to take the Monday off, you can."

"No Bob. This is too important. I will be back."

"Shall we reconvene here on Monday at nine a.m. then?"

As if man proposes and God disposes, PG interjected, "Can we make it at seven a.m. instead?"

"I don't see why not...is there any particular reason?"

"No, I just want it to get it done and close this chapter for good."

"Any objections?" Bob posed the question to Priya and Simrin.

They shook their heads indicating there was none.

"OK, we'll meet at seven on Monday, week after next. Tomorrow being Friday, let's gets a head start."

"Aren't you heading to London?"

"Yes, I'll be with Betty and the kids, and I'll fly back on Sunday morning."

"I thought that Betty was flying Monday morning?"

"I'll let them keep their original tickets and schedule."

"I will fly the late flight from Chicago on Sunday," said Priya.

"I will just relax in my pool at the apartment complex." Poor Simrin had to add her two-cents worth, while explaining her poor state of affairs.

Bob immediately reacted and said, "Simrin, after this production, with your cut you will be able to afford a big house in my neighborhood. I would love to have you move there."

PG took leave of them and left. Priya and Simrin straightened their desks and were soon on the way out. Bob was just getting ready to go out himself and shouted, "Have a good vacation you two!"

Priya and Simrin looked at each other as they headed towards the elevator.

The late August sun was setting in the western sky. It had an ominous glow attached to it. It was blood red and rather ghastly. The sun seemed to have a red face, indicating he knew what was in the future. Time had its own beat—it wanted to slow down. People in the Big Apple were heading home in their own merry ways. Cars fought for their rightful space on the highways. A bunch of Broadway producers contemplated a revival of *The Teahouse of the August Moon*. The sky was impatient to be filled with the blue moonlight and abundance of stars. Why do people on Earth, knowing that there are billions of stars and billions of planets billions of light-years apart, still insist on being the center of attention on an egotistical ride that is finite. The whole life of an individual equates to a fraction of a second in the universal time continuum, and we think we are it.

There was a blue hue that surrounded the vicinity. The only distracting and wrong notes in nature's symphony were the electric lights and the noise of cars. The Statue of Liberty was standing majestically, shining a guiding light to incoming ships.

The color blue has a serenity associated with it. It's the color of the universe, as we perceive it from Earth.

Why do they call feeling melancholy, the blues?

Chapter Twenty-One

It was Sunday morning.

The sun started to peep through the large trees in Hyde Park. People were jogging, and the pigeons were waiting for their benefactors to come and feed them. Suzie and Sam made it a point to feed the pigeons every morning. It was their ritual. As usual, they went out, sat on the bench, and started to feed the pigeons. The pigeons were not at all bashful. They hovered over the two of them with absolutely no fear and were the personification of what freedom was. The thought comes to mind, are they as complicated as the human species is?

Sam and Suzie were sitting very quietly. Suddenly, as if he could not control himself any longer, Sam blurted out, "Suzie, there's something different about Dad."

Suzie did not answer but she felt the same way. There was something distinctly different about their dad. She could not pinpoint what it was. She was very much afraid that it might be a precursor to something that was going to happen. She remembered her friend's dad, who had suddenly become very loving to his family. He was trying to hide behind the façade he'd put up, in order to keep suspicion away from his encounters with this young beautiful damsel he'd been having an affair with. Suzie tried very hard to calm herself down. She was trying to convince herself that it was not true and that it was a figment of her imagination. She looked at Sam.

"Isn't there?" Sam asked her again.

Though she was the older one, Suzie did not know how to react or what to say.

There was a very attractive brunette jogging down the path. Sam and Suzie saw her coming. She came close to them and panting, stopped to take a breather. "Good morning, Suzie," she said.

"Good morning, how was your trip to India?"

"Just fine, how was your UK jaunt?" Then the woman added," Hi Sam, you look troubled."

Sam didn't know what to say. Yes, he was troubled. He didn't know what to think about his dad. Suzie was also in a quandary. Both their faces spoke volumes.

Kathyayanee was very good at understanding youngsters. That was her job, teaching at the university. She had to figure out what her students were thinking and get into their minds, to answer questions, clear doubts, and comfort them, all while educating them. She knew there was something bothering these two.

For Sam and Suzie, she was a stranger they'd met on the plane on their way to England. She had become quite a good friend to their mother. The two women had hit it off as if they were bosom buddies.

Seeing the kids' expressions, Kathyayanee figured out what was happening in a split second. Some people have this special knack of reading people's minds. She was good at it. She also knew that if you pry too much, people won't talk. So she kept her calm. Turning to Suzie, she said, "Life here in Europe is calm and peaceful, isn't it?"

Usually when someone is in a troubled state you talk about peaceful things. This prompts them to open up, trying to seek that which is peaceful. Suzie was puzzled, but felt an urge to discuss their apprehension with Kathyayanee since she was a stranger and would not have pre-conceived notions about the subject matter. "We are kind of worried."

"Worried?"

Silence prevailed as if Suzie was reassessing if she should confide in Kat or just let it pass. Kat knew exactly what was happening and waited for her to sort out her thoughts herself.

Suzie looked straight into Kat's eyes as if she was evaluating her integrity and wisdom. After a brief silence both kids turned towards her. "We see a change in our father," said Suzie.

Sam added, "He is completely different."

"He is more considerate and loving."

"There is something absolutely different."

There was a lull. Kat understood that the "why" of the sudden change was bothering them.

"My friend's dad used it as a camouflage to hide his affair with a younger girl. In the end, he divorced her mother."

Both kids were really puzzled and troubled and they wanted to get feedback.

"So you are afraid that your father is putting a show."

"Precisely like playing a scene from a movie," said Suzie miserably.

"Why don't you ask him?"

"He might get very angry and go back to his moods."

"So you like him as he is now and you don't want him to change, but you are afraid that he might leave your mother. Am I right?"

"Right on."

"You should quietly ask your father what's the actual matter. Let him know that you are concerned."

"Do you think he'll answer?"

"There are two possibilities."

"What are they?"

"If he is having an affair, then he will get annoyed that the cat is out of the bag."

This sent a chill through Sam and Suzie. They wondered if they should have ventured to ask Kat about this "cat." Suzie remembered Kat joking with her mother about an encounter in the waiting area at the airport. Suddenly she had a suspicion. Was Kat the other woman? Suzie felt stupid that she'd asked her for help. But since they *had* asked her they had to put up with it.

"On the other hand..." said Kat.

"What?" said Sam.

"Tell us. What?" Suzie asked urgently.

They both were very anxious to understand Kat's thinking and deductions. Kat figured out that she had created a tense moment by choosing the wrong words earlier. She had to make amends. "On the other hand, his change in behavior might have been prompted by a change of philosophy, because he was affected by a story or some happening that changed his outlook for the better."

"Like a born again..." mused Suzie.

Kat cut in. "No, that is a change to a dogmatic belief. That's not what I mean. I mean a change in philosophy, in understanding what the Universe really is."

"You mean a greater understanding."

"Yes, when the *Challenger* disaster occurred, there were a lot of people who stepped back to revisit their lives and their concepts of how fragile life is on this Earth."

"You are telling us that our dad changed because he had something happen to him that made him rethink life?" asked Suzie.

"That may be it…he was working on that story for the movie. Just ask him, he will tell you."

The kids were relieved. As she was about to start back on her jogging path, Kat said, "There is no cat in the bag. The mind plays weird games with you. You have to clear your thinking once in a while. Give the mind a good shower and a soapy wash."

"It *was* playing games with us," said Suzie with a smile.

"Confronting problems with a soft touch is what is required to ease a lot of family problems and global problems as well." Kat got back to her jogging, leaving the two kids to make up their minds about they were going to do.

Suzie took Sam's hand and said, "Let's go and ask him."

They walked back to the hotel and entered the lobby where the bellboy greeted them. "I just delivered breakfast to the room."

"Thank you."

Sam and Suzie waltzed up the winding stairs of the hotel. Ironically, it was the same room PG and Julia had been in for their anniversary. The bellboy was the same one who had delivered flowers to Julia. This bedroom suite seemed to have the flair of uniting lovers in exotic settings. Wouldn't you like to be a fly on the wall? As the two kids entered the room, Bob and Betty were dressed and having breakfast.

"Kids, we're going to take an open-top tour bus ride of London. Would you like to join us?" asked Bob with a smile.

Suzie was figuring out how she was going to approach the change of subject. This looked like an opportunity not to be missed, so she answered, "Depends on how you answer my question."

"Go ahead and shoot the question."

"We notice a change in you."

Bob had been expecting this and so had Betty. She hadn't wanted to ask Bob herself because it would have made her look as if she did not know her own husband. She was glad the kids had solved her dilemma.

"I was going to share it with you." Bob started to figure out how he was going to approach this, as Betty and company anxiously awaited hearing the story. "As you know, I was working on a project."

"Kanishka," said Sam.

"Yes. The writer, PG, spent a lot of time explaining the trials and tribulations of two families who suffered great losses. Hearing the story, I came to understand what a family really means. How interdependent we are, and how much support we need from each other."

There were tears from all of them.

"I realized that in this world, as long as we live, the only thing that is more precious than life itself is family. And the fertilizer to a good family relationship is unquestioned love and a lot of it."

The three of them looked at him with an unknown feeling of affection and love.

"I have missed a lot of years without knowing the true meaning of love," he said. He looked at Suzie and Sam. "It's not launching someone in the back seat of an MG."

Sam and Suzie were experiencing a new soft-spoken dad with a logical explanation for their question.

"That's lust. Love is to take care of someone whom you have chosen to spend the rest of your life with. Children are the fruits of such love to cherish forever."

There was no movement in the room. Every one of them stared at Bob in admiration and amazement. So much change—they wanted to meet that author to kiss his feet and thank him.

"So what is your verdict?"

"Dad. You and mommy go have fun."

"Yes Dad."

The kids rushed to him and hugged him. That was probably the first time they'd ever hugged their dad. All their love had been coming from their mother. Father had only been a provider, but now, suddenly he was accessible. Bob hugged them both and Betty joined in the huggathon.

"I just want to spend some quiet time with Mom. I'm flying back today at two for my meeting tomorrow."

"You both go and have some time alone, Dad. Sam and I will go to Shepherd Market and have that pizza. We'll be back in time to see you off to the airport."

Bob and Betty got up and were on their way as the clock struck nine. "Kids, we'll be back by twelve," said Betty.

"OK Mom."

Bob said something that was not usual. "We love you kids."

The two walked out hand in hand to catch the bus. Sam and Suzie were relieved and happy that they'd asked Kat what to do.

Bob held Betty close to him as they sat in the last row of the open upper deck of the London tour bus. The two smooched and whispered sweet nothings to each other. All the other tourists were jealous. The bus was finding its way through the busy London streets. Betty had always wanted to do this, but Bob had never found time to do it before. He was always so busy that he couldn't spare the time. Now he understood what he was missing.

Some people have it and don't know it.

Some people have it and don't use it.

Some people have it and still don't have it.

Love is a complicated four-letter word, isn't it?

The whole family went to Heathrow Airport in one of those London cabs. All through the ride, the kids watched their parents hold hands. Love had manifested in the Stevenson household.

"Why don't you travel with us tomorrow morning?" suggested Betty.

"I set the meeting very early and should be there."

"I am going to miss you."

"I am too. You will be coming early-morning tomorrow anyway. We'll have lunch with PG. He is a nice chap as the British say."

Bob gave Betty a big passionate kiss and walked away into the customs line to catch his flight. Both kids were happy to see family values get reinforced. It was not that they hadn't existed; they had been dormant in the subliminal thought process.

They just needed a nudge.

Back at the hotel the three of them had evening dinner together.

"I miss Dad," said Sam.

"So do I," said Suzie.

Betty thought to herself, *He is no longer a provider but a sustainer.* She said aloud, "Let's walk down to Royal Albert Hall and see if there is a program that we can watch."

The city of London never sleeps. I guess royalty made sure no one slept at nights. They needed company in merry making.

Later that night, the telephone rang in the room. Betty answered, "Hello."

"It's 10:30, time to leave for the airport, ma'am."

"Make sure we have a taxi for the airport."

"OK ma'am."

"Kids, it's time to go."

The call was all that was needed. Everyone went down and took the cab to the airport. They rushed to the ticket counter, checked in the luggage, and passed through customs to the secure area in the airport. Betty, for some unknown reason, was slowly attracted to the store that sold ties. She felt compelled to buy a tie with small elephants on it.

The clerk there asked her, "You are an American, aren't you?"

"Yes. Why do you ask?"

"I remember another American bought this same tie."

"Is that right?"

"I remember it well."

"What?"

"I asked her if she was buying it for her boyfriend."

"And?"

"She asked me why I thought it was a boyfriend."

"Why *did* you think it was a boyfriend?"

"I made the mistake of thinking that Americans were all promiscuous."

"Don't they teach you how to behave with customers?"

"She gave me a piece of her mind in a pure British accent."

"Why do you remember that now?"

"She selected the same tie with elephants."

"Will you please put it in a box and wrap it?"

"Do you want to write a note?"

"Yes I do."

The girl gave Betty a note pad and pen, and as she was completing a note for Bob, someone tapped her on the shoulder. She turned around to see Kat.

"Kat! How was your trip to India?"

"Just fine. How was your vacation?"

"The last week was just picture perfect."

"Did Bob join you?"

"He did, and you have got to hear this."

Just then Sam and Suzie walked into the store with Cadbury chocolates in their hands and in their mouths. As soon as they saw Kat, they rushed to her and hugged her as if they'd known her forever. Betty was puzzled.

Kat knew exactly what had happened.

"Just like you advised, we asked him," said Suzie.

Kat just laughed. Betty was still puzzled, but Kat came to the rescue. "I met the kids in Hyde Park. They were worried unnecessarily. I said to them that the best way to solve a problem is to confront it with a soft touch."

Betty immediately knew what had prompted the kids' question to Bob. In the innermost depths of her heart, Betty had also been concerned. Not having an extended family to depend on has a lot of ills attached to it, notwithstanding the ills that can be associated with an extended family. Betty had been hoping that she would meet Kathyayani to ask her for her advice. She was happy it was already accomplished. She suddenly, unconsciously hugged Kat.

The kids gave her a chocolate and the four of them slowly walked toward the departure gate where the jumbo 747 jet was majestically waiting to take the passengers on the trans-Atlantic flight to John Fitzgerald Kennedy Airport in the United States.

All the passengers got onto the plane and it rolled off to its takeoff runway. The four engines roared and the big beast started to run down the taxiway at an enormous speed. The wind that blew and gusted past the wings was diverted by the front edge of the wing to the topside. This created a vacuum that sucked the wing into it and along with the wing, the whole plane lifted itself into the suspended level and started to ascend. Its flight path was to the north across Scotland, then Ireland, then Iceland, and onto Canada. From the north, Newfoundland, and down over Maine and Boston into New York's JFK Airport.

The plane was racing against the sun. The sun had started to peep into the United Kingdom when the flight took to the air and flew towards New York where the time was five hours behind. The sun was right behind, following the flight path of the plane.

As the giant 747 was about to land at JFK, the time was 6.45 a.m. The sun kept pace with the plane and started to rise in the eastern sky.

As usual, when Bob got to his office building, he started to climb the stairs. As the 6:55 mark arrived, Priya, Simrin, and PG met at the elevator and proceeded to join Bob. As soon as Bob took his brief shower and changed, the foursome met in the conference room.

The meeting was called to order with everyone holding their coffee mugs but PG, who had his soft drink. Bob got up and asked Priya and Simrin to follow him into his office. The three disappeared for a short while.

PG wondered what had happened. He played with his tie. It was red with tiny elephants on it, just like the one that Betty had bought for Bob.

The three of them waltzed back into the conference room and Bob started to address the task at hand. "I'm sorry that we just had a huddle."

"It's OK."

"I had to get everyone on the same page."

"I understand."

"We are all very excited about your work and are very happy that you chose us over all the others in this field."

Priya butted in, "Is there something which you would like to let us in on, such as your priorities and expectations?" She was trying to offset any gaps in expectations with what Bob was willing to deliver. In defense of Bob, he was being over-generous with PG.

Bob understood what Priya was doing, and waited for PG to answer the question.

PG got up from his chair, walked around the table to the big picture window, and started to slowly open the blinds. As the three of them watched him, they realized that he was not his grubby self as before, but was well dressed and sporting a red tie with elephants on it. He was very confident in his moves. He seemed to have overcome the shadows of his past.

Everyone understood that John was none other than PG and Joanna was none other than his wife Julia, and the kids were his own Abe and Rose. They all had chills. Bob suddenly picked up his cell phone and called JFK flight-arrival information to ascertain that the flight from London to JFK had landed safely. He felt relieved.

PG, in his confident composure, just waited till Bob was through with his phone call. He moved back to his chair and started to talk. "Thank you Priya, for asking me that question. People have a tendency to take things for granted. You guys have realized that the story was not fiction. Everything happened."

There was complete silence from everyone.

"Rohit was my friend—he lost everything also. His wife and kids. We both lost everything only three years apart. For me, the writer, I experienced the same thing I was writing about. Bob, you asked me why I went AWOL on you. Did I have a choice?"

Bob shrugged his shoulders, Priya was uncomfortable, and Simrin just took it in.

PG continued, "Priya, you asked if I had any priorities…Yes, to let the world know what these terrorist attacks do. How they hurt people in far-off places. Like that grand old man, Rammayya garu." He looked at Bob and continued. "We Americans are programmed right from the beginning to believe that we are always right. Sometimes we do not care to understand another man's point of view. Arrogance, it may be. As much as we pride ourselves, we just are not responsive to other people's culture and civilizations."

Bob was lost for a moment and didn't know where PG was heading with this spiel.

"That's why I want Priya to direct this. She understands and appreciates the Eastern way of thinking as well as the American way of interpreting. That's my second priority."

As he was thumbing through his copy of the script, Simrin walked out to her office and retrieved her copy from the filing cabinet before rejoining the group.

PG noted, "I have only one copy of this script, and with the four copies you made, we have only five all together. Keep them safe. Bob, you have the fiduciary responsibility for this screenplay to be made into a movie."

Bob was speechless. He finally got the courage to say, "PG, I am willing to give you anything you want for this masterpiece."

PG thanked him. "Priya, I have here the consent and waiver from my friend Dr. Rao, the grand old lady Seethamma, and myself, giving you all rights and copyrights for this script for publication and movie adaptation." He handed over a folded piece of paper to Priya. "Put it in the inner pocket of your jacket."

Priya looked at Bob and he nodded. She took the paper and put it in the inner pocket of the jacket she was wearing.

PG looked at Simrin and smiled. "Simrin, you are just like Mamta and Julia. You are very compassionate. You like to take care of people. You want to be remembered as one who helped a lot of people. You helped me a lot to get through these few days. I have something for you."

"I don't need anything."

"No. This is something special."

The curiosity was mounting. What was he going to give her? He pulled out a tie box and a wrapper with a bow attached to it. Giving it to her he said, "This is what Julia wrote to me before she was taken away from me. It was destined for me to get it. I need this to be preserved. I am sure you will take care of this for me."

"What am I going to do with this?"

"Save it. If the movie ever gets made, let this be the last thing the audience sees."

Simrin held it close to her and put the letter into the inner pocket of her jacket.

Suddenly, there was a big thud as if there had been an earthquake, along with a phenomenal rise in temperature. Everyone was suddenly sweating.

There were no more sounds and it was calm for a while. The temperature became comfortable again. Bob took the opportunity to bring out his agreement. He gave it to PG and started to explain, "I left a blank for the fee for your script. I would like you to fill the amount in as whatever you want."

"Bob, as I said, Priya is the copyright owner. She should decide what a fair amount should be."

Both looked at Priya. Priya did not know how to wiggle out of this predicament. She ventured, "The highest amount we have ever paid for an option is five hundred thousand. Would that be a reasonable amount?"

PG smiled…

"Am I out of line?" she asked.

"No, you have recommended the maximum, how can you be out of line?"

"OK, we will make it seven hundred and fifty thousand dollars," Bob blurted out.

"Bob it's yours…don't outbid yourself, " laughed PG.

"I'm sorry. I just want to please you."

"I know. Will you make the check payable to the Harmony Foundation?"

"What is that?"

"It's a foundation to teach and propagate inter-religious tolerance and understanding. All the terrorist attacks are mainly due to religious intolerance."

The time was 8.50 a.m. There were sounds of all sorts of sirens. Priya went out to explore, followed by Simrin. She looked out of a window and saw the adjacent building was on fire. Rushing into the conference room, she said, "Bob, the next building is on fire. I am going to investigate, please get ready to evacuate."

Priya and Simrin went to the elevator, took it down and walked out to the front where they started seeing what was happening.

They saw people jumping to escape the smoke and fire that was raging through the 94th to 98th floor of the building. Close to two hundred people dropped down from the sky like raindrops. How desperate they must have been. The watch on Priya's wrist indicated 8:55.

She was affected by the human shower of bodies hitting the concrete slab at the bottom, shattering blood all over the area. While some experts were claiming that their building was safe, she reached for her cell phone and called up to Bob. "Bob you've got to come down immediately and see what is happening. Both of you please come down immediately. My instinct tells me that is not safe to be there with this adjacent building on fire."

Priya said to Simrin, "In these kinds of situations, my dad always asked me not to put myself in compromising situations. We should follow our instincts not procedures."

Time has this peculiar habit of not stopping for anyone. The seconds ticked and minutes passed. They were like hours with no end in sight.

Priya and Simrin anxiously waited for Bob and PG to come down. The building next door was still burning and people were still jumping out of the top windows.

It was two minutes to nine.

Priya called up again; this time it was on the speakerphone. "Bob, what the hell are you doing? Get the hell out of there and come down you dumb fool…"

"Bob let's go down immediately." So saying, PG got up and proceeded toward the elevator lobby. Bob, as usual, headed towards the stairs for his exercise and started to run down. At the elevator bank, PG pressed the down button. He had now overcome his fears and come to terms with life's perversities. For through the big glass vista windows across from the lobby, he saw an airplane flying too low in the southwestern sky. He straightened the watch on his wrist and saw it was showing 9:00. The elevators took minutes to climb up to the eightieth floor.

The elevator came up and stopped. The doors opened and there were lot of people on it. One of the passengers shouted, "Get in and let's go."

PG got in and turned right around. There was a roar of jet engines. The sound was increasing. It reached a high decibel level. The elevator door was struggling to close. There were people obstructing the electronic eye. Everyone was trying to pile in. Through the window they saw a plane. It banked at an angle and was on a collision course. The elevator doors were half closed. The jet engine sound was deafening. The nose of the aircraft broke the glass panes. It had a force that was immense. It crushed all the elevator passengers.

The elevator was on its way down. The plane's impact had broken the cables and the elevator car came crashing down, already mangled with the impact.

Betty, the kids, and Kat shared a taxi from JFK. They were talking about their vacations. The cabbie switched on the radio with a comment, "The towers are on fire."

Betty and Kat reacted. "What towers?"

"WTC towers."

The news was on the airways.

"Recapping the breaking news. This morning, a hijacked American Airlines jet carrying ninety-two people hit the north tower of the World Trade Center at 8.46. a.m. The jet struck the ninety-fourth through ninety-seventh floors. Many people on those floors were instantly killed by the impact. With all escape routes destroyed and no other alternative, many jumped off of the top floors. Please stand by. We have some breaking news coming in…Oh… No…Oh…God…we have just received news through unconfirmed sources that a second United Airlines jet has hit the south tower of the World Trade Center approximately between the seventy-fifth to the eighty-fifth floors. Again, repeating, at 9.03 a second hijacked jet hit the south tower. Smoke is pouring out of the two towers. We are being reassured that there is no danger and that the buildings are safe."

"Get us to the towers, Bob works there."

"So does my sister Priya," Kat announced.

"Dad works on the eighty-first floor."

"Priya is your sister?" asked Betty in surprise.

"Yes, get us there fast."

The taxicab started to speed and race towards the two towers that seemed like two big, over-sized chimneys spouting smoke as if from an atomic plant.

Meanwhile, Bob was already at the seventieth floor when he heard the big bang and explosion above him. He looked up to find a huge ball of fire traveling down the stairwell. He spotted a shower of water coming down too and surmised it to be the sprinkler system trying to douse the fire. He'd started to climb back up to help people when the sprinkling drops hit him and he realized it was not water but looked and felt like kerosene. He figured it was aviation fuel and that it was not wise for him to go up. He turned back and started to climb down the stairs.

Pandemonium struck and all the people started to head to the elevators and found that the shafts were acting like transmitters of smoke and fire. The only option was to go down the stairs. They were all doused with aviation fuel.

Bob spotted an old lady in a wheelchair trying to figure out what she was going to do and how she was going to get to the bottom. It looked as if the elevators were out of service.

Bob went her, asked her to forget the wheelchair, put her on his back and started his climb down the stairs. On his way down he saw a few more people stranded. By this time the firemen had started to climb up the stairs with their equipment. Bob was carrying this lady and fighting his way down while the firemen were fighting their way up. He emerged through the downstairs double glass doors at 9.40 a.m.

Priya and Simrin spotted Bob and were glad he made it. Bob just left the lady there, asking someone to get her out, and again went back into the building to help the stranded people on the fiftieth floor. His adrenaline was flowing and when he got there, he again picked up an old frightened old lady and started to bring her down. The temperature in the building was unbearable. In places it was close to 1800 deg F, fueled by the aviation jet fuel. The steel of the buildings had withstood the impacts created by two 767 Boeing jets traveling at speeds of 450-590 mph. But they'd had full fuel loads and the building supports were now getting weak. Steel melts at temperatures of close to 2450 F. It also quickly deteriorates in strength at elevated temperatures. It started to show signs of buckling. Bob immediately recognized the danger. Minutes looked like hours. It was 9.55 and Bob was on the twelfth-floor level.

Priya just could not take the torture anymore, decided to go in and fetch Bob out of the building, and started to do so. Simrin held her back and tried to persuade her to wait just for five minutes. Priya looked up and started to notice some kind of movement. Simrin felt it too.

"Priya, it's coming down."

They stared at the building. Coming down, Bob started to hear a rumble and guessed that it was time and that the building was coming down any minute.

The taxi came to a stop approximately five blocks away from where the towers were located. Only police and fire trucks were allowed anywhere near the towering infernos. Kat, Betty and the kids got out and started to run towards the towers. Volunteer workers stopped the four two blocks from the towers.

"My husband Bob works in the south tower."

"My sister Priya also works there."

"We have to find our dad."

The volunteer refused to let them go any farther.

The time was 9.59.04

Bob was at the door of the stairwell with the lady he was carrying. He had to go round the elevator shafts and to the outside exit door where Priya and Simrin were standing.

It was so close yet so far.

Priya and Simrin saw the building start to crumble before their own eyes. They did not see Bob come out. The building collapsed. There was a huge dust ball that engulfed the whole area. It was like the "Aandhi" dust storms. One cannot see through them.

The dust storm moved through all the streets and people started to run away from the tower area to be safe. As everyone were running away, including the volunteers, four people ran into the dust storm shouting the names… "Bob – Dad – Daddy – Priya!"

Priya and Simrin were the only two who stood through the storm in anticipation of finding their boss. As the dust surrounded them, they moved back from the building and tucked themselves into a cozy corner of the adjacent building.

The progress of the four was slowed by the dust storm, which took about twenty-five minutes to settle down. The four were anxious not only for their kith and kin but also for each other since they got separated.

Betty broke down. Her mind was going crazy. Now she felt she'd lost her kids along with her husband. She started to shout hysterically for them. Kat joined her in shouting for Priya at the top of her lungs.

Priya heard the shouts and responded. Tracking by where the sound emitted, the four of them and Priya found each other. "Priya are you OK?" Kat enquired anxiously, as Betty was making sure that her kids were OK. After she had hugged them, Betty turned to Priya and said, "Don't tell me Bob didn't make it."

"He went back into help," Priya replied in a quiet voice.

As they all watched, the north tower collapsed at 10.28.31. The ball of dust started again. No one could see anything. The six of them held hands and did not separate through the dust storm.

They decided they would all shout at the top of their voice and call out for Bob and PG.

"Bob…PG…We are here."

"Bob…PG…We are here."

"Bob…PG…We are here."

"Bob…PG…We are here."

"Bob…PG…We are here."

"Bob…PG…We are here."

Through the dust a figure showed up, carrying someone on his back. "Betty, Sam, Suzie."

They ran to him and hugged him. "Thank God you are OK."

Bob looked for Priya and Simrin. "Did PG make it?"

"No…planes and he don't get along."

They all felt as though they'd lost a close friend.

For five blocks they walked, sobbing and hoping that by some miracle they would find PG. The taxicab was waiting there for them. Kat took her luggage out of the cab.

Betty and the kids got in the back seat of the cab and Bob sat beside the driver. He saw Priya and Simrin still sobbing for PG.

Bob got out of the cab and hugged Priya and Simrin. Then he looked at Kathyayani and took her into the fold. "He said it was my fiduciary responsibility to take care of his script…I failed…I just saved his option check."

Priya and Simrin looked at him with blank faces.

"I failed him… I failed him."

Weeping, Simrin looked at him and said, "No you didn't fail him."

Everyone looked at her.

"I left my copy at home and it is safe."

~

The dust settled and plans for the rebuilding of the towers started. The second anniversary rolled by.

RLS Productions released its motion picture, based on a story by the late PG Woodward. It was directed by Priya and produced by Simrin, and at the end, after the roll of the credits, was the letter Julia had written:

Dear PG,
As long as our memories last
Death does not us part.
Julia

Did he orchestrate his end?

Lightning Source UK Ltd.
Milton Keynes UK
UKHW010943060821
388423UK00002B/323